AF486346

UNDER THE MILKY WAY

A BLUEBIRD BASIN NOVELLA

JESS K HARDY

Copyright © 2026 by Jess K Hardy

All rights reserved.

This is a work of fiction. Names, characters, places, and incidents either are the product of the author's imagination or are used fictitiously. Any resemblance to actual persons, living or dead, events, or locales is entirely coincidental.

No part of this book may be reproduced in any form or by any electronic or mechanical means, including by AI or machine learning algorithms, including information storage and retrieval systems, without the express written permission of the copyright holder. Unauthorized use, including the use of any AI or automated systems to analyze, replicate, or generate content based on this work, is strictly prohibited.

Edited by: VB Edits

Cover design by Jess K Hardy

Published by Pinkity Publishing LLC

A NOTE TO READERS

This book contains discussions of children going off to college. If you, like me, cry a little whenever you think about your 17 year old leaving home, take care. Also, Darryn has been deployed in the past and this is also discussed.

*For everyone brave enough to ask,
and everyone brave enough to say yes*

CHAPTER ONE

HANNAH

WHY WAS the cow in the middle of the road?

No, this wasn't the beginning of a dad joke. This was my life.

"Hey, Siri." I tapped my fingernails on the steering wheel, staring at the big brown cow as it stared right back at me. "Call Stephanie."

"Hannah, babe," Steph chirped after two rings. "How was the flight?"

"Oh, fine," I said, still tapping. "A little bumpy on the descent, but fine."

"And the drive?" she asked.

"Long, but very pretty. A couple things, though. One, where on god's green earth are you sending me? I'm thirty miles from the Canadian border."

"You brought your passport, right?"

"What?" I balked. "No, I did not bring my fucking passport—"

"Chill," she said, far too amused at my expense. "I'm not sending you to Canada. Just about as close as you can get without meeting a Mountie. What's the other thing?"

"Well." Rolling my window down, I waved my arm in the air. The cow only chewed its cud, its big black eyes peering straight into my soul. "There's a cow in the middle of the road. A whole-ass cow, just standing there."

"Open range is a trip, huh?" She said it like this was all completely normal. Like bovine roadblocks were everyday occurrences way up here in northwestern Montana. And, shit, maybe they were. What did I know?

"How do I move this thing? Do I need to call someone?"

"Who? The cow police?" Papers rustled across the line. "Have you tried honking?"

"I have. Twice."

"Yes, but did you honk with purpose? You must *mean* it, Hannah. The cow will know if you don't." She muttered something to someone, and I clearly heard the words *incident report* and *intervention*.

"Are you still at work?" It was already seven o'clock here, six in Sequim. "Steph, it's Friday night. Get out of there."

"Can't." She sighed the collective fuck-my-life sigh of every high school counselor stuck late at their desk cleaning up other people's messes. "School year is getting off to a hell of a start. We had two fights, a sub walked out after fourth, and we just found a veritable brick of weed in a sophomore's locker. Seriously, we could build a house with it. Just drive. It'll get out of your way."

"The weed?" I joked.

"That weed isn't getting out of anyone's way."

Wincing at the brown mass of hair, horns, and muscle now pawing at the ground in what looked like annoyance, I said, "I think you might be underestimating this particular cow. He's an absolute unit. What if he kicks my car or headbutts a headlight? I doubt free-range livestock damage is covered under the rental insurance."

"Nah," she dismissed with a certainty I wasn't sure she'd earned. Hadn't she grown up in Boston? And suddenly she was a cow whisperer? "The worst it'll do is take a dump on your hood."

"Pretty sure that's not covered either." Taking a deep, fortifying breath, I put the car into drive. "Okay, I'm moving."

"Good for you. It's like losing your virginity," she said. "Inch by inch, babe. Inch by inch."

"Don't remind me," I muttered as my tires popped over the dirt road. "Jimmy Conway. He cried the entire time. Nobody came."

Steph gave that comment an "oof" while the cow whipped its tail through the air, mooed with deep and mournful disdain, and finally pivoted out of my way. Not, however, before giving me a thoroughly unimpressed side-eye that put my students' best efforts to shame.

"I'm through," I said.

"Proud of you," she slurred, probably gnawing on her pen the way she did when she was stressed. "It's actually good you called when you did, because if you're that close to Canada, you're about to lose cell service."

"I am?"

"Yep."

"What, for like a few miles?" I glanced through my windshield at the trees, the mountains, the sky, since—not counting the cow—that's all there was up here.

"Uh, sure," she said. "Well, maybe a *bit* more than a few."

The beginnings of a shiver buzzed along the base of my neck. "Steph?"

"Actually, you will not have cell service for the rest of the miles to town. And for all the miles surrounding your cabin."

"What?" It came out as a shrill yelp. I picked up my phone, the sharp tang of adrenaline flooding me as I watched three bars shrink to two. And then there was only one. One lonely bar struggling to hold it all together, which, at the moment, felt a little on the nose.

"Don't panic," Steph said. "I explained it all in the directions I drew you. And I've already told William and everyone here that you'll be off grid for the next few days."

"Off grid?" I looked in my rearview, ready to turn around. But the damn cow was back, blocking the road again like some cloven-hooved Gandalf. "What do you mean 'off grid'?"

"You know," she said, like it was obvious, "off grid. As in the opposite of on grid. As in not reliant on public utilities like water or electricity."

Panic flared inside my chest. "Is this some weird Gen Z thing? You're all nostalgic for when life was hard and everyone died of dysentery?"

She only laughed.

"This isn't funny, Steph."

"Don't sell yourself short, Hannah. That was very funny."

The steering wheel creaked under my grip. "Please tell me you aren't sending me to a fucking cabin in Middlefuck, Montana, all by myself, without electricity."

"Okay, I won't." A pause. "Even though that's what I'm doing. And it's called Balsam Ridge. Not Middlefuck. Although I love your creativity."

I groaned.

"Hey, you asked me for this, remember? You sat me down and asked for my help. You told me, your favorite coworker in the entire world, that you needed somewhere to disappear for a few days. And this is it. *This* is where you disappear. Jane and I stayed in the same cabin last summer, and it changed our lives. That's not hyperbole, by the way. PeePaw's Hideaway is so cute and cozy—"

"PeePaw's?" I cut in while my mind conjured an image of a wrinkled old man waiting for me at the front door wearing faded overalls and a floppy hat. Probably missing some teeth.

She ignored me. "And you are going to *love* the little town and the mountains and the sky and the stars if you just unclench your spleen for, like, five seconds and take a breath."

"My spleen is not clenched," I insisted through a jaw that most certainly was. Squinting up at the rapidly darkening sky, I said, "And it looks like it's about to rain, so I don't know about seeing any stars."

"Hannah, you need a fucking break. You agreed to trust me, so trust me."

I blew out a heavy breath. She was right. I did need a break, and I had agreed to let her plan this trip. But still… "I don't even have a flashlight. How am I going to survive without electricity?"

"Yes, you do. It's in the bag I packed for you. You've got everything you're going to need up there. And the cabin has propane, so you'll have lights and a stove and stuff."

Well, that was better than nothing. "But there's no cell service? At all?"

"Ugh, fine," she relented. "The General has Wi-Fi."

"The who?"

"It's a little tourist store. But I strongly encourage you not to spend the entire weekend hunkered down there mainlining coffee and doomscrolling."

"I don't doomscroll," I lied. "I just like to watch reels of babies eating their lunches. It soothes me."

"Let it all go for a few days, even the babies eating their lunches. It will be fine. I promise. Everything will still be here when you get back."

Actually, everything wouldn't still be there when I got back. And that was the problem. That was why I'd wanted to disappear in the first place. Because William was already gone. He was off to college, and being alone—which was something I hadn't been in eighteen years—was no longer my strong suit.

It's funny how a person can be so completely unaware of how their lives have changed them. I never had a problem with being alone before I became a mom. I loved it, actually. I was good at it. But then, out of nowhere, you wake up one morning, walk down the stairs, and stand in the middle of a house so catastrophically silent it feels less like an empty nest and more like an abandoned tomb. And you realize that you are not the same. You realize that you can't bear the silence. You realize that you would rather talk to your furniture than not talk at all. And after a few days of talking to your furniture, you realize that you need to figure your shit out before you wind up self-committing to inpatient psych.

So that's what this weekend was for. That's what I needed. To go somewhere quiet and peaceful where I was surrounded by pretty things. Where I could learn how to be alone again. I just didn't expect Steph to take the request quite so literally.

"Okay." I gathered myself together with a sharp sniff. "You're right. This is exactly what I asked you for." *Even if I never imagined that road-blocking cows would be involved.* "I'll give it a chance."

"Good," Steph said firmly. "Oh, and make sure to...if you... open—"

"Steph?" My voice rose as hers faded, my palms turning clammy. "You're breaking up."

"Follow...directions," she said, ghostlike through the static. "Make sure...look up...stars."

And then she was gone, and I was alone. Again.

CHAPTER TWO

HANNAH

IN TEN MORE ZERO-BARS MILES, I reached the town of Balsam Ridge. If you could call a dirt road, a saloon, and a general store a town. But I had to give it to Steph, it was beautiful here.

Mountains towered into the moody gray sky, their rocky peaks ringed by larches and aspens whose leaves were just starting to change. It was that time of year when summer green was a breath away from exploding into golden fall. The change was already in the air, crisp and nostalgic, like the smell of a favorite sweater when it was finally cold enough to pull it out of the closet. Even though I'd never been here before, this place felt nostalgic too.

A sharp pang pierced my chest when I drove by a group of kids playing volleyball outside their cabins while their parents watched, drinking beer and eating burgers at their picnic tables. It was like looking at a painting, a memory, an entire life moving away from me while I could only watch it go.

Thunder rumbled overhead, and I left the boundary of the little town to follow Steph's hand-drawn directions, turning left at the "big-ass tree" three dirt roads past the General, then a right after the

"Prince-purple" mailbox, and then a quarter mile down a tree-lined drive toward my final destination.

As I navigated the deeply rutted road, two words corkscrewed through my mind, twisting my belly: Off grid.

Until that moment, I'd only known the words as a theoretical concept, something for survivalist communes or reality TV shows. But there was nothing theoretical about PeePaw's Hideaway—so designated by the wooden sign swinging on its hinges at the end of the drive.

Rustic with a capital R, the small two-story cabin was covered in weathered cedar siding, topped by a roof so mismatched I wondered if it had been installed in stages over the years, and the rickety front porch looked like a great place to get tetanus.

When I parked the car and killed the engine, cutting my audiobook off mid-sentence, I stepped outside, and a profound silence swept in around me. It was the kind of quiet the old me had loved. A break from the noise of daily life. No horns honking or trains clattering, no sirens shrieking or students shouting. Today, though, the silence was too loud, too big, a deafening black hole sucking me in, making my skin pull tight and the hairs on the back of my neck stand on end. And maybe I didn't want to be alone all weekend. Maybe I couldn't do it. Maybe this whole thing was a huge mistake.

But then I closed my eyes and took a breath, then another. And little by little, soft sounds came to me, nature filling the void. Birds trilled in the trees. Crickets sang in the grass. A creek burbled gently around the property as a metallic, pre-rain breeze stirred the gauzy white curtains in the cabin's open windows. Because why wouldn't the windows be open all the way out here? In a place where cows outnumbered people? Where families played volleyball while surrounded by unspoiled beauty? Where crickets sang and creeks burbled? Where I stood frozen in the middle of a driveway?

"Come on, Hannah," I muttered to myself. "You can do this."

Pulling my carry-on bag from the back seat, I made my way gingerly up the warped porch steps. I punched in the combo Steph had written down for the lock box by the door and frowned when I flipped the lid open and found nothing inside.

"Well, shit."

After checking the ground for the key—even shining my phone's flashlight through the porch slats in case it had fallen through—and not finding it, I called Steph. A call that, of course, went nowhere because there was no service.

"Shit, shit, shit."

A dog barked, and I jumped. It sounded close, but there were no other cabins nearby. No tails wagging in the long grass. When the dog barked again, I realized it was *very* close, and my head whipped back toward the door.

"Hello?" I knocked softly on the weathered wood. "Is someone in there?"

Paws clicked in an excited scramble, followed by the thud of heavy footsteps. Check-in was two hours ago, but maybe someone was still getting the cabin ready. That happened sometimes, right? Maybe I was about to meet the infamous PeePaw.

But when the knob turned and the door swung open, there were no faded overalls, no floppy hats, and definitely no missing teeth. There was only a man. A man who appeared to be about my age. A man wearing a half smile, a towel, and nothing else.

Tall, was a word my mind managed to pull from a sea of white noise. More words arrived shortly thereafter: *curly wet hair, broad shoulders, a bare chest. That tiny white towel clinging to strong, capable hips.*

"Hello."

His voice was deeper than it had any right to be. His eyes bluer. Jaw more defined. Silvery stubble fresher. Like he'd left his razor at home because a clean shave had no purpose in a place like this.

"Oh, are you..." My brain was so insistent on the absurdity of asking him this question that I could barely make myself say, "PeePaw?"

Amusement radiated from him. "Not quite. Can I help you?"

"Well, um..." My attention wandered from the patch of dark curls covering his pecs to the patch of even darker curls shading the valley between his abs. When a soft whine drew my attention farther down, between the man's slightly spread legs, I found the dog sitting at his bare feet. It was a scruffy little thing. Some kind of pug mix, maybe, with a coarse black and silver coat, an adorably smushed face, and enormous round eyes that stared hopefully up at me. They reminded me of William's when he was a toddler. When he'd reach up with his chubby little arms and ask, "Carry you, me?"

A fist gripped my heart.

"Are you all right?" the man asked when I hadn't managed more than a *well, um.* "Do you need help?"

"No. I'm sorry." I only realized I was digging the heel of my palm into my chest by the way his brow furrowed when he noticed it. "I..." I dropped my hand. "I must be at the wrong cabin."

But even as I said it, I knew it wasn't true. The key code had worked. Steph's directions had been immaculate. And the sign was kind of a dead giveaway.

I wasn't at the wrong cabin. He was.

"I mean, is this," I cleared my throat and asked, "PeePaw's Hideaway?"

His lips twitched. "The one and only."

"Okay," I said slowly. "So, are you leaving today?" My gaze meandered, unbidden, back down to his towel. "Maybe late for checkout because you were taking a shower?"

Crossing his arms over his chest, he leaned against the doorframe. His eyes, crinkling at the corners, kind of *sparkled* at me. "No shower. This cabin doesn't have running water."

"But...you're all wet."

He pushed his tongue against his cheek, fighting a smile, and I felt a sudden desire to dive headfirst into the creek behind us and let it burble me all the way to the ocean.

"I wasn't planning on leaving today," he said with something that felt like generational calm, like if he had them, his siblings were calm too. And his parents and grandparents. Unbothered all the way back to hunter-gatherer times. "I'm booked through Monday."

"You're... Just you?" I asked for some unknowable reason. "I mean, you're here alone all weekend?" *Good god!* "I mean *I* am here alone all weekend," I finally got out. "This is my cabin. My coworker rented it for me."

"Wait." His brows slid together over his glacier-blue eyes. "Are you serious?"

I pressed my lips into a tight *well I'm certainly not joking* smile.

"Shit." He rubbed at his stubble. "PeePaw must have accidentally double-booked us. I reserved this cabin last year. And the year before that. I stay here every Labor Day weekend."

The smoke from the cognitive grenade of seeing a gorgeous nearly naked man in a cabin I thought would be empty began to clear, and my heart, putting it all together, slumped against my ribs.

This wasn't my rental. This wasn't my weekend to get away from it all and find myself again. It was his.

Despite the tears threatening to sting my eyes and blur my vision, I refused to cry in front of this bare-chested, deep-voiced, generationally calm stranger. But I really needed one thing in my life to go right. Just one.

"Got it," I said before spinning on my heel and marching back to my car.

"Hey." He came after me, walking to the end of the porch. Which, with that porch and his bare feet, seemed ill-advised. "Where are you going?"

"To find somewhere to sleep tonight. Sorry to bother you. Enjoy your stay."

When I started back down the drive, he remained in my rearview, standing in his towel, watching me go with a concerned expression while his dog dropped a tennis ball at his feet and a light rain began to fall.

⋆ ⁕ ⸳ ⸱ ⸳ ⸳ ⁺

"Can I please get access to your Wi-Fi?" I begged through a ragged breath after barreling into the General.

"Storm caught you out, huh?" the twenty-something cashier behind the counter asked. "Here." Their eyebrow ring glinted as they handed me a towel with an intricately tattooed hand.

"Thank you. Wi-Fi?" I asked again, drying my face and neck as rain pelted the windows, rain that transitioned from a light sprinkling to a biblical downpour once I was back in town.

"Sure. It's $4.99."

"You charge for your—" I cut myself off. "Of course you do. Why wouldn't you? We're a captive audience here. Like a cruise ship that goes absolutely nowhere."

They winced. "I know, right? But you do get lifetime access, so…" Trailing off at my expression, which probably conveyed at least twenty different ways of saying *do you honestly think I am ever coming back here?* they took my card.

After paying for the Wi-Fi—and a huckleberry cinnamon roll because I was a stress-eater and they smelled amazing—I tucked myself into a corner. Surrounded by chocolate bars, tourist hats, and Montana history and travel books, I pulled up Steph's contact.

"How did I know you'd be on the Wi-Fi within ten minutes of getting there?" she asked by way of hello. "Seriously—"

"There is a man in my cabin."

"Damn, woman." She whistled. "That might be a land-speed record for finding a hookup. I am so proud of you right now."

"No, Steph." I pinched the bridge of my nose. "Not a man for me." Although I might have considered it for 0.5 seconds after watching a droplet of water slide down his throat and settle into the divot above his collarbone. "A man who also rented PeePaw's Hideaway for the weekend. We were double-booked, and he got there first."

"Oh. Shit. Oh no," she said, the gravity of the situation finally setting in. Almost. "Wait, what does he look like? Is he hot?"

"Steph!"

"You're right. Sorry, sorry. But now that you're mentioning this, I do remember thinking it was kind of wild that the cabin was available, because literally everything else up there was booked. But I thought it was kismet, you know? Like it was meant to be. You and Balsam Ridge and that one perfect cabin."

"Did you just say that everything else was booked?" I sounded like a steel guitar, high-pitched and whiny. "Because it's getting late, and it's raining, and I don't have anywhere to stay."

"Okay. Don't panic. It's going to be all right, I promise. I am going to figure this out for you." Her stern *get the fuck out of my way and let me work* voice at least allowed me to breathe again. If anyone could fix this situation, it was Steph. Last year she successfully deescalated a love-triangle breakup that included a brutal diss track, six furious parents, and two squad cars on campus. "Give me ten minutes. I'll call you right back."

Sliding my phone into my purse, I walked back to the counter.

"Any chance there's a hotel around here?" I asked the cashier. "Someone is apparently already staying at my rental."

"I kinda overheard," they said while ruffling their pixie cut. "What a bummer. I'm pretty sure the entire town is booked up. Holiday weekend, ya know? But you might find something in Garnet Springs."

"That's two hours from here." I wanted to weep. After flying and driving all day, I just wanted to sit by the fire in my slippers and stare into the void until I passed out.

"Yeah." Their nod was solemn, understanding, like a doctor telling a bread lover they had to stop eating gluten. "We offer free camping out back, though. I think there are still some spots available, if you have a tent."

Even though the cabin had no running water or electricity, I highly doubted Steph included a tent in her "everything you're going to need up there" bag.

Lightning flashed, followed by a crack of thunder so loud it shook the windows. And fuck a tent.

Handing the towel back to the clerk, I said, "I'm not really a camp in a thunderstorm kind of gal." I rubbed my arms as adrenaline drained from my bloodstream, leaving me cold and wet and hollow. I needed to get warm, then I could figure my life out. I needed dry clothes, a sweatshirt. There was one in my carry-on, I just needed to go get—

Time slowed, and like the second hand of a clock, my head ticked toward the window. Toward the parking lot, where my car was, but my carry-on bag was not. Because I'd left it on that bare-chested man's front porch. "Oh, fuck my entire fucking life."

"Good luck," the cashier called out as I shoved the door open, ducked my head, and stomped back out into the rain.

When had this happened? When had my life become such a diabolical cosmic joke? I used to be on top of shit, totally in control. I was a mother, a wife, a professional and put-together person. Now, I was a lonely, single, forty-six-year-old disaster who did things like leave her bag on stranger's porches.

Driving way too fast back down the dirt road that was more of a muddy river at this point, I turned left at the big ass tree, right at Prince's mailbox, and then jerked hard into my seat belt when a rut in PeePaw's driveway swallowed my front tire.

Making a keening, high-pitched, and completely unhinged sound, I threw the car in reverse, then rocked it forward again. Not budging physically, but spiraling at lightspeed emotionally, I stomped on the gas pedal and gunned it. My wheels spun in a futile shrieking whir, fat clumps of mud painting the windows while the car burrowed itself deeper and deeper into the earth. There was a metaphor in there somewhere, but I'd be damned if I'd acknowledge it now.

Surrendering to the fact that the only direction I seemed to be going was down, I killed the engine, shouldered the door open, staggered out into the rain, and promptly lost a shoe to the wet, sucking mud. While I hopped one-footed toward the cabin, shouting curse words at the sky, some distant part of me knew that my tenuous grip on sanity had slipped. That the loneliness creeping up behind me all week had finally sunk its teeth in.

By the time I dragged myself up the porch steps, the rain had plastered strands of my hair to my face, my clothes clung wetly to my body, and I could barely breathe through the viselike grip cinching my chest. Hot tears made tracks through the cold rain on my cheeks, and when he pulled the door open before I'd even raised my fist to knock, when he stood there in a snug white T-shirt and loose gray sweatpants with his mouth half open and his brow half creased, I lost the fight, hung my head, and started to bawl.

CHAPTER THREE

DARRYN

It stressed me out when anyone cried, on a deep, visceral, I-have-to-fix-this-now kind of level. But there was something about a beautiful woman crying two feet in front of me that really fucked me up, every tear making my eye twitch and my brain growl, "Who hurt you and where can I find them?"

"I'm s-sorry," she stammered through a body-wrenching sob that clenched my hands at my sides. "But I just flew all day, drove here in a rental car that has decided to fossilize itself in the driveway, made it through a live cow roadblock, and lost one of my favorite shoes in the mud to come here for what was supposed to be a relaxing getaway. So I could at least try to reset after a really shitty week that included"—she raised her hand to start counting on her fingers—"totaling my car, flooding my basement, getting my first colonoscopy, talking down one of my sophomores after he let me know, in the middle of the hallway, on the first day of school, that he was freaking out because his girl-friend wanted to peg him."

Do not laugh, Darryn. This is not funny.

"And then"—she pulled in a jagged breath and, okay, now I could relax a little. At least she was breathing—"and then my son, my favorite person in the whole entire world, decided to leave for college a full week early because he wanted to hang at the beach with his buds instead of hanging with me, his mother, who's loved and supported him unconditionally his entire life, who's been his 'bud' since the day I pushed him out of my body and into the world."

Ah, and now it all made sense. I'd been there too once and remembered that particular ache. I couldn't fix what was hurting her. But I could listen. So I nodded, encouraging.

"And now," she sobbed, "I have to come to terms with the fact that he's gone. That I won't be making him breakfast or dinner or getting us surprise iced chai lattes on random afternoons. I won't be able to hug him every morning or listen to him play his guitar after school or watch TV with him every night."

While she spoke, I wondered if she was putting her feelings into words in real time, like maybe she hadn't said these things out loud yet. Maybe, because I was a stranger, I was safe to say them to. If only she knew how well I understood her, the way each word hit me like a punch to the gut. If only she knew how badly I needed to get her inside and out of the rain.

But when I opened my mouth and extended my hand, she blurted out, "I won't know if he's okay or not." Tears streamed down her cheeks. Tears I wished I could brush away with my thumbs. "Because he's such a stoic kid," she went on, still wet, still cold, still crying. "And when he's home, I can see it. I can tell when he's struggling. But what if I can't tell when he's gone? What if he never calls me? What if he gets annoyed with me and stops answering my texts? What if we slowly just"—her chin wobbled—"drift apart? I don't know what it's going to be like. I don't know what our relationship will turn into. All I know is that he's gone. And I am so completely and utterly and unbearably alone—"

Okay, that's enough.

"Christ," I bit out. It was an explosion of a word, like pressurized lava finally bursting through the rock holding it back. "Get in here." Taking her hand in mine, I pulled her into the cabin, into my arms.

"Shh," I whispered into her soft, dark hair that smelled like rain and coconut. "It's going to be all right. Just breathe, okay?" I held her close as she shivered and shook and gasped for air. "Take one breath for me. Just one."

But she only wept, and it felt like one of those cries that had been building up for so long there was nothing left to do but wait until it was done. So I slid my hand under her hair, squeezed her neck and said, "I've got you. I'm here. You're not alone."

She wrapped her arms around me, her hands fisting in the back of my shirt, and she was so cold. But when I loosened my grip on her and said, "You're wet. We need to warm you up," she shook her head against my chest and clung to me.

"Okay, okay." I wrapped her up in my arms again, tucking her head beneath my chin, ready to hold her like that as long as she needed. "I understand."

Her tears still came, soaking my shirt. But slowly, with each degree of heat that transferred from my body to hers, her shivering faded.

"That's it," I said, deep and calming. "Just breathe. Nice and slow. Like this." I took a breath, nice and slow. She took the next one with me. "There you go," I soothed.

While her tears faded, we rocked in a slow dance to no music, her fists opening, her palms pressing into my back, fingertips curling over the muscles along my spine.

She smelled so sweet, like the end of summer. And when I cradled her head, when her breath ghosted over my neck, pebbling my skin, before my brain could remind me that I didn't even know this woman, I said, "That's my good girl."

She froze in my arms. And, shit, I'd really done it now, gone too far like I always did. I was about to apologize when her face tilted up to mine, her mouth hovering just above my collarbone, her eyes trained on a spot on my throat that every nerve ending in my body sprinted for like a gold medal was on the line.

Her fingers closed, gathering my shirt between them, pulling.

And as her breath stuttered, as she leaned in close, as my heart tumbled over its next beat, I thought, *what the fuck is happening?*

And then, answering my unspoken question, she pressed a kiss to the side of my throat.

I swallowed beneath her lips, my pulse pounding as my hand on her neck squeezed and pulled until she had no choice but to look up at me. As my other hand at her back urged her closer, pressing her softness into where I was growing exceedingly hard through my sweatpants.

We stared. We breathed. We crackled like the electrical storm still churning outside as something beyond words passed between us, some primal understanding flashing in her clear deep brown eyes. And while I studied her fair skin, freckled nose, red lips, long, nearly black hair. While I wondered what those red lips might taste like, feel like against mine, she started to say, "I need..."

I sensed her searching for the end of the statement. And maybe she wasn't sure what she needed. Or maybe that was it. Maybe simply needing was enough. Because right then, I needed too.

Taking her face between my hands, I brushed my thumbs softly over her cheeks, drying her tears the way I'd been dying to since she showed up crying. "What can I do?" I asked. "How can I help?" She only stared at me, her big brown eyes still glistening. But I, *we*, wouldn't do what I thought we might be about to do without her express permission. "Tell me."

"I..." She trailed off, tried again. "I..." A gasp cut her short this time when I dropped my hand to her ass. Just to help. Because it seemed like she might need some help. "I need...that. More. Please."

Under that please, the long, drawn-out pleading of it, I heard: *Please read my mind. Please don't make me say it. Please just know.*

And even though what I was about to suggest seemed absolutely bonkers, I was cool with it. I was a risk taker. Always ready to jump. You only regret the shots you don't take, right?

So I squeezed the round globe of heaven in my palm and asked, "Do you need to be fucked?"

Her eyes popped, her mouth forming the most perfect little O. But it was her single nod that was all I needed to pick her up, hook her legs around my waist, and turn toward my bedroom.

While she started kissing my neck, I pulled off her remaining muddy shoe and tossed it down onto the mat. She licked the spot behind my ear that always made me shiver, and when I wrapped her cold and wet foot inside my warm, dry hand, she whimpered.

Fuck, that sound. It shot straight to my dick. I wasn't sure I'd ever been so hard in my nearly fifty years on this earth, which was, honestly, kind of amazing.

Mouthing, "Stay put" at my dog over my shoulder, I pushed the bedroom door open, then kicked it shut behind us. When I laid her down on the bed, she scooted back toward the pillows, her wide eyes watching me wrench my shirt over my head. Crawling up onto the bed with her, I slipped the button of her pants free and slid them off. But when I pulled her legs apart, licked my lips, and pressed a hot, open-mouthed kiss onto her underwear, she grasped my face and pulled me up.

"No," she said. "No foreplay. Just... Please."

Staring forlornly between her thighs like she'd just taken away my favorite dessert—because she had—I sighed, then nodded. This was more about her than it was about me. I could live without licking her, tasting her, even if I'd probably fantasize about it for the rest of my life.

Backing off the end of the bed, I stood and pushed down my sweats and boxer briefs. And because she was watching with full-moon eyes, I pumped my erection with a slow, lazy fist. Once, twice, and when she whimpered again, my cock throbbed in my hand. I needed to be inside her. Now.

Crawling over her again, I pulled her up long enough to take off her shirt and unclasp her bra, then I tossed both over my shoulder. Reaching into my nightstand drawer, I grabbed a condom from the box I never left home without. I tore the wrapper open with my teeth and asked, "Can I touch you?" while I rolled the condom on. She didn't want foreplay, but I still needed to make sure she was wet. "I don't want to hurt you."

She nodded, and her eyes fluttered closed when I reached between her legs, cupping her soft heat in my palm. I swept my fingers through her slick core and slid them over her clit, and when she bit back a moan, I wanted to stay there all day, making her come over and over with my fingers and my tongue. I wanted to slow down, to savor her, to push away the moment we'd wake up from this dream and she'd come to, realize what she'd done, and probably snatch up her clothes and run.

When I slid a finger inside her, just the tip, she said, "Oh god," on a breathy exhale that heated my blood.

"Will you tell me how you like it?" I asked. I knew I only had one chance at this, and I wasn't going to fuck it up by guessing. "How you need it?"

"Hard," she said while I brought my slippery finger back up to graze her clit. Her back bowed off the bed, her perfect breasts rising into the air. I wanted to spend hours there too, maybe even days, kissing and licking and sucking her nipples into my mouth. But she had other plans. "Now."

Yes, ma'am.

Nestling between her thighs, I took myself in hand, positioned my head at her entrance, and met her stare. When she nodded again, I pushed inside her with one slow, determined thrust.

Fuck, the sound she made. The way she gripped me. The heat of her body as she tilted her hips and spread her thighs wider. This was bad. I mean, it was amazing. But I was in dangerous waters, barely keeping my head above the surface of the orgasm building in my tightening balls. And if there was one thing I wasn't about to do, it was come before she did. No fucking way.

What was it Mattie had told us he used to imagine when he was trying to hold out? When we were young and siphoning as much intel as we could from our older and wiser brother? Goblins? Trolls? No, leprechauns.

Leprechauns, Darryn. Think of leprechauns.

She gasped, grasping my shoulders as I drove into her, hard, just like she'd asked. I did it again and again, finding a rhythm, even if it took every ounce of strength I had to keep myself together.

Creepy leprechauns. Evil leprechauns. Dancing leprechauns. For some reason, that last one worked.

Finally far enough from the edge that I trusted myself to give her what she needed for longer than five seconds, I settled my weight over her and asked, "Can I kiss you?" while my hips rocked, while I hooked my arm under her knee, pulling, opening her up.

"Yes," she hissed after a particularly hard thrust. I'd angled that one a little bit too, and I couldn't help my smug smirk when her inner walls flickered around me and her fingernails dug into my shoulders so hard I knew they'd leave marks.

Leaning forward, never losing my rhythm, I kissed one corner of her mouth and then the other, light, soft, teasing. When I brushed my tongue over the seam of her lips, she opened for me, and I swept inside. She tasted like huckleberries and mint, so fresh and sweet, and somehow, I kept my kisses slow and patient, even as I drove into her so hard the headboard marked the time in sharp, staccato thuds.

She broke off the kiss, catching her breath as her eyes opened, finding mine. Fuck, she was sexy. When her chest heaved like that, her lips parting, her walls closing in around me.

Touching my forehead to hers, I brought a hand up to cup her breast. "Are you close?" I asked, flicking my thumb over her nipple.

"Maybe," she said, almost a whine. And when I angled my hips again, pinched and rolled her nipple between my thumb and finger, she pulled me down into another searing kiss.

"Hmm," I hummed, soothing her with my voice as my hips and the headboard continued their unforgiving pace. "I think so. I think you're close."

She nodded, and I told her, "You feel so good. You deserve this. You deserve to feel good too. Can I touch your clit? Can I rub it and make you come? I want to feel you squeezing me, so hot and tight."

"Yes."

The word was barely out of her mouth when I shifted to the side and reached down between our bodies. When my thumb found her clit and circled, slow at first, gentle, she sighed, but there was a bite to it.

Circling faster, I gave her a little more pressure. And then I pulled back and tried to catch my breath. Because this was all just a little too perfect. Her full lips, her chest rising and falling, her breasts pressing into me as she arched her back. And when I pressed down a little harder, pushed into her a little more deeply, kissed her while she came apart beneath me, that was the only word repeating itself in my mind: perfect, perfect, perfect.

I could have lived buried deep inside her, fucking her like this all night. She was so wet, gripping me so tightly in pulsing waves, and so fucking gorgeous as she came down. But it was her smile, the first one I'd seen on her, that yanked me back to the edge so hard I had to gnash my teeth to keep from tumbling over it.

"Your body," I said, straining, still moving, still hovering, trying my hardest not to fall. Not yet. "Your body has done so many amazing things. And right now, it's all for me. What a gift." I cupped her breast, brought her nipple to my mouth, and sucked. Even then, I kept moving, kept thrusting, kept my pace. "All this soft skin and these perfect curves. So fucking sexy. So fucking...*fuck*," I gritted out when she canted her hips, grabbed my ass with one hand and my neck with the other, and hurled me off the cliff.

My head dipped, my chin dropping to my chest as sensation gathered in the base of my spine, coiled in my stomach, twisting tighter and tighter at her cries and her lips on my skin and her teeth sinking into my shoulder, until it broke free of my grip, ecstasy barreling through me, hot and bright and draining me dry.

CHAPTER FOUR

HANNAH

*O*H. *My. God.*

His head was on my chest, and while I panted into his hair, I wondered, did that just happen? Was any of it real? Was it all a dream? Had I hit my head on the steering wheel when my car slid into the rut? Had the last hour been just some absurdly hot hallucination?

It must have been. I must *still* be dreaming. Sex like that didn't happen in real life. Not to me.

But his body, the human-blanket weight of him pressing me into the bed, it didn't feel like a hallucination. The skin of his back, warm and soft under my hands, his firm muscles and ragged breaths, they didn't feel like a dream. The sensation of comfort that seemed to seep from his pores, that was intensely real.

When he rolled to the side to remove the condom, then rolled back to nestle against me, I cradled him in my arms as the rain fell, tapping against the windows in the otherwise silent room.

Until his fingers dipped between my legs again, brushing over hyper-sensitive skin, and I said, "No. It's too much. I can't."

"I know." He cupped me, firm but gentle, a steady pressure. "It's just…you're so soft." The words seemed to pain him. "So warm. I just want to touch you." Sliding his fingers over me, around me, everywhere but the place I was still swollen and tender, he said, "Just for a little while longer."

Even though I was wrung out, the aftershocks of the orgasm he'd given me still pulsing deep in my belly, my clit gave an interested flicker, and I told him, "Okay."

He was so slow and careful. And I let myself sink into the luxury of being caressed by someone because they thought I was soft. Because they wanted to touch me when it had been a very long time since anyone else had. So many years since I'd been explored by curious hands like this. I'd almost forgotten how this kind of attention could feel, the significance of lazy fingers trailing over my skin, mapping my curves, learning my shape. The sense that my body could be a place to spend time, something to appreciate, to savor. A cathedral instead of a drive-through.

And when his mouth started exploring me too, his lips trailing kisses over my shoulder, my neck, my breasts while his fingers pushed inside me and pulled out again, painting my wetness over my inner thighs, my labia, my perinium, outlining my entrance, making my skin shiver and tingle everywhere but where I was suddenly, desperately aching for him, I remembered this too. How easy it was for me to come like this, without pressure, without expectation, with only attention.

His lips closed around my nipple, his tongue swirling, and heat surged through me, pooled between my legs, making me moan, making me reach for his hand and guide him to my clit.

He released my nipple with a soft chuckle, like he knew exactly what he was doing to me, like it was all by design. His warm breath ghosted over my wet skin as he moved his finger up and down over my clit, still slow, still careful. It was torture, in a way. His steadiness, the way he'd already brought me to the edge, and now held me suspended in a pleasure so intense it felt close to pain.

"Please," I said, and then again, softer but even more desperate, "Please."

He liked that, the pleading, and rewarded me with a bit more pressure.

"You must be a dream," he murmured against my skin, his fingers moving so slowly that each pass over my clit made my body jerk and my breath hitch. "Like I wished for you. Conjured you from thin air."

I couldn't hold on, couldn't survive here much longer, my body so deeply attuned to the pad of his finger that I swore I could feel the distinct swirls of his fingerprint. It was too good, too bright and sharp and hot. And when a single tear tracked down my temple, when I trembled and gasped and begged him again, he took mercy on me.

Taking my nipple back into his mouth, sucking and licking and grazing his teeth, he circled his fingers just fast enough, just hard enough, that despite the rain, despite the clouds and the roof over our heads, I saw stars. A million motes of light burning brightly behind my eyelids as pleasure broke over me, sucked me under, drowning me in deep, unrelenting waves.

When I finally came up for air, he kissed me, and I tried to kiss him back, but I was so tired, so relaxed, so rubbery when everything inside me had been tense and tight for so long that I'd forgotten there was any other way to feel. My eyelids drooped. My arms, heavy and useless, sank to the mattress. And when his head came to rest on my chest again, the smell of woods and rain lulled me to sleep.

✦ ✦ ✦ ✦

THERE WAS a scratch at the door. A soft bark. A deep voice mumbling, "Just a second, Joey."

Joey? Who's Joey?

My eyes cracked open to a dark room, an unfamiliar ceiling arching above me, unfamiliar wood paneled walls surrounding me.

And a door, also wood, with a... I squinted. Yep, that was definitely a deer antler for a handle. What the hell? Where was I—

An electric bolt of panic shot through me as I flew upright, memories of hands and lips and orgasms hitting me like a thousand volts to the chest.

"Holy shit!" My clothes? Where the fuck were my clothes? "Holy fucking shit!"

"Don't freak out," that deep voice mumbled again. He blindly patted his nightstand until he found the lantern lamp and clicked it on. "I think we both needed that."

"Don't freak out?" I repeated, incredulous as my heart rammed into my ribs and the lamplight illuminated his messy hair and hooded eyes in a muted orange glow. "You want me to not freak out that I just fucked a complete and total stranger in the middle of the goddamned wilderness?" What was I thinking? He could be a serial killer. A very skilled and talented serial killer who smelled like the forest. "I'm losing my mind. That's it." Finding my pants, I shoved my legs inside them, backward at first—because, of course—before I ripped them off and tried again. "The stress was too much," I said. "And I broke, that's all. I broke and lost my mind, and where the fuck is my bra?"

"Leave it." His voice was all gravel, raspy and deep. "You have phenomenal tits."

"Oh my god," I wheezed, spinning in a frantic circle. "I have to get out of here. I have to go."

He rubbed his eyes before checking his watch, which he promptly removed and set on his nightstand. "We fell asleep. It's after midnight." He tilted his head, listening to the drumming on the roof. "And it's still raining. You should stay."

Meeting his stare head on, I said, "I am not staying with some"—I waved my hand up and down at him—"*man* I don't even know."

"Oh, you kind of know me." There was a far too amused tilt to his lips. "In a biblical sense."

"That was..." Spotting my shirt next to the bed, I yanked it over my head. He could keep the bra. "I had a lapse."

"A lapse?"

"Yes." Tugging my shirt straight, I hauled my attention up from his flat abs, his broad chest. "A lapse in judgment."

He sucked in a wounded breath, his hand rising to land in a patch of soft, curly chest hair I knew the precise feel of against my breasts. "Ouch."

"Well, I..." I'd started strong, then lost steam when he raised a brow at me, folding his other hand behind his head, waiting with that unflappable calmness for me to form a thought. "Um, thank you...for your...services." It was as poetic as anything I'd ever said. "And goodbye."

"Wait. Don't go." He sat up, leaned forward, suddenly serious. "The roads up here wash out in the rain. And your car is already stuck. Please stay. There's another room upstairs. You did pay for this cabin too, after all." With a hesitant shrug, he offered, "We could share it."

I blinked at him. "You want to share it?"

Raising his hands at my wary expression, he said, "Look, I'm sure you've heard this before from men who weren't, but I'm a good guy. I promise. I actually felt terrible when you left. I was waiting for you to come back for your bag so I could give you the cabin. I have a tent, and I figured I could either pop it somewhere on the property or camp behind the General. But then you were so sad and cold."

And you fucked me unconscious. "Can I have the cabin now?" I asked.

His big shoulders fell by a fraction, barely noticeable. "Is that what you want?"

My mouth opened, then closed again. The truth was, I didn't know what I wanted. Part of me wanted this, him, more of whatever had just happened between us. So much more. And another part of me, the smart part, the careful and reasonable part, wanted to run away as fast as my legs would take me. Because I didn't do this sort of thing. I didn't have one-night stands with auburn-haired and blue-eyed strangers. I didn't let that same stranger give me multiple orgasms while making me believe I'd deserved each one. Like they'd been my birthright. I didn't, because he—this—it was a trap. A taste of life that had no basis in reality. Something I would compare to everything else that ever happened to me from this day forward and say *nope, not good enough, might as well pack it in because you've peaked.*

"I don't know," I answered eventually, honestly. "I don't know what I want."

"What if we slept on it tonight?" he suggested. "And if you still want us to leave in the morning, Joey and I will go. Is that reasonable?"

I pulled in a slow breath, then let it out. Waiting until morning was, I had to admit, quite reasonable. Because aside from generational calm, this was obviously another of his strong suits. Being reasonable. And being absolutely spectacular in bed. But that was neither here nor there...

"Okay." Finally spotting my bra and underwear hiding under a corner of the bed, I scooped them up and gathered them to my chest. "We'll decide in the morning."

Giving me a triumphant grin that curled my toes, he said, "Good. But before you go, I have to know. What's your name?"

I groaned, nearly dropping my underwear when I palmed my face. We'd kissed, fucked, held each other, fallen asleep together. But I still didn't know his name, and he didn't know mine. Who even was I anymore? "It's Hannah," I said, resisting the urge to do something ridiculous like hold out my hand for a shake. "Hannah James."

Reclining back onto his pillow, his right hand resuming its position on his chest while his left slipped behind his head again, he said, "Hi, Hannah James. I'm Darryn Madigan. It's been *very* nice to meet you."

A sharp bark at the door saved me from having to respond.

"That's Joey," he said. "My dog. He probably needs to go out."

"He's not the only one," I muttered as my bladder twinged. "Is there a bathroom around here somewhere?"

"Ah, no." He scratched the back of his head. The gesture was apologetic, almost boyish. Adorable. "But there is an outhouse." Swinging his long legs over the side of the bed, he leaned forward to pull on his sweats. And while I checked out his perfectly round butt, I repeated, dryly, "An outhouse."

"I know." He tossed a sleepy grin at me over his shoulder. "But believe it or not, it's actually pretty charming."

I did not, in fact, believe it. But it was either give it a try or pee in the woods in the dark. No thank you. Besides, huddling close to him under his umbrella, with his arm wrapped around my waist as he ushered me down a sloshy, pine needle-lined path, wasn't so bad.

After passing a firepit on one side and a hammock strung between two trees on the other, there, in the rain-streaked beam of his flashlight, appeared a roughhewn wood shack no bigger than a dorm room closet.

I squinted at it, because it certainly didn't look charming. But then he pulled the door open, reached inside to flick on a set of battery powered string lights, and said, "Welcome to PeePaw's pride and joy."

"Oh, wow."

The outhouse walls were painted navy blue and yellow gold, a starry night sky with a crescent-moon shaped ventilation hole cut into the back wall. The string lights twinkled along the ceiling, and the toilet bench was clean and smooth and decorated with lavender sprigs, skiing and hiking magazines, and a plastic container holding two rolls of toilet paper with a picture of a mouse inside a *no* symbol painted on the top. It didn't even smell bad.

"Have you actually met PeePaw?" I asked, turning back toward Darryn.

The twinkle lights reflected in his eyes, filling them with glittering stars. "Of course."

"What's he like?"

Moving in close, he reached out, ran his fingers down a strand of my hair, and said, "Short."

It was just cold enough that my huffed laugh misted into the air between us.

"He's in his eighties," Darryn continued, dropping his hand to his side. "Sweet guy. He still works as an accountant in Garnet Springs. Still comes up here all the time to make improvements on the cabin. He must have swapped out all the propane lamps this year because they're all new. I keep offering to come over in the off season and help him." His lips twitched. "He always says no. Stubborn old goat."

"He sounds great," I said, staring at Darryn's mouth.

After a moment of staring at mine too, he toed at the ground. "Well, I should probably stop keeping you from..." He tilted his chin toward the outhouse

"Right," I said awkwardly. Then I spun around, about to venture into PeePaw's pride and joy, when he asked, "Hey, Hannah?"

I turned back.

"Do you feel better? Better than you did?"

It was really unfair that trying not to blush just made the blush even worse. "Um, yes," I admitted, because I did feel better. Better than I had in years. "Thank you."

"You're welcome." When he dragged his lower lip between his teeth, my knees wobbled. "And if you want to feel better again, all you have to do is ask."

With my mouth open and eyes wide, I felt like a fish. I must have looked like one too, because his nostrils flared as he tried not to laugh at me.

"Here." He shook out the umbrella, closed it up, and set it in a little tin bucket by the door. Then he passed me the flashlight. "For your walk back."

The handle was warm from his grip, and I wondered what that was like, always being warm, exuding heat like a furnace. "What about you?" I asked while raindrops fell into his hair.

Stepping back, holding his arms out wide and angling his chin toward the sky, he said, "Don't worry about me. I *love* getting wet."

As much as his head scratch before had been boyish, my giggle was equally girlish.

"See you in the morning?" There was a note of hope in his voice, but some wariness there too. Like he was already imagining waking up and finding me gone.

And maybe that would have been the smart move, to get out with my dignity somewhat intact. But when I cut a sideways glance to my car, which the earth seemed to be actively swallowing whole, I realized how unlikely a rapid exit was.

Stepping into the outhouse, which was impossible to do gracefully, I said, "I'll be here." Then I closed the door, surrounding myself with twinkling string lights and the sound of rain falling on the tin roof, three words repeating themselves in my mind: holy fucking shit.

CHAPTER FIVE

DARRYN

I FLIPPED the strips of bacon in the pan, letting them sizzle. It didn't matter how tired I was—and she'd worn me out plenty last night—I always woke before the sun. Holdover from my years in the service. And while I was more than happy to let her sleep in, it was almost nine, and I was a little desperate to see those deep brown eyes again. So I broke out the big guns. Because even though the coffee I'd brewed hadn't done the trick, nobody could sleep through the salty aroma of fresh bacon on the griddle.

Or Joey's high-pitched bark when he smelled it too.

"Shh, buddy. Let's let her sleep," I said for show, winking at him while I tossed him a piece. When I heard her feet land softly on the floor above me, I tossed him another one and whispered, "Good boy."

He wagged his tail, chewing happily before rising onto his hind legs, asking for more. But when her door creaked open, he forgot all about the bacon and raced up the stairs to greet her. Couldn't really blame him there.

My nerves buzzed when she said good morning to my dog. When she told him he was such a handsome little rascal, that buzz transformed into a full-body zing. How would she be this morning? Would she be chill? Would she want to leave as soon as she could? Would she have regrets? I fucking hoped not. I'd deal with it if she did, but— *Shit, here she comes. Game time.*

I tried to play it cool, just a normal, relaxed guy making morning-after breakfast. But then she stepped into view at the top of the half staircase wearing slouchy, cream-colored socks over black leggings and a light green hoodie that barely brushed her hips. Her dark hair twisted up into a bun with soft strands brushing her neck, and suddenly *cool* was no longer on the menu. How could it be when she looked so hot? Like, burn-your-hand-if-you-touched-her hot?

But that wasn't even what really got me. What got me, what made the cabin seem twice as bright and the bacon smell twice as good, was that she looked comfortable. I didn't want to get my hopes up, but she looked like a person who might be interested in bumming around a cabin in the woods all day with a guy she'd just met.

"Morning," I said, giving her my best smile, the one that tugged at the right corner of my mouth more than the left, the one that made it all the way to my eyes. The one that used to kill when I was younger. While I wondered if it still worked, she stopped walking mid-step, and her cheeks flushed a pretty rose.

Almost fifty, but I still got a few tricks left.

"Morning." She took me in, her gaze sliding up from my favorite faded jeans that hugged my ass to the dark gray Evergreen State College T-shirt that hugged my biceps. It was the third outfit I'd tried on before leaving my room this morning. Not that she ever needed to know how pressed I was to look good for her.

"Sleep well?" I asked.

"I did," she said. And wow, yeah, okay. If we were playing smile chess, she just knocked my king across the room. Because her best was a hell of a lot better than mine. So good that those pink lips and the little dimple in her cheek hit me like a kick to the ribs, stealing my breath. But wait, was that even her best? Were there more? There had to be. Who knew how big her arsenal of smiles was. I bet there was one in there that would take me to my knees. And now, along with convincing her to stay, I had a second goal for the weekend: find that smile.

"I didn't really notice it last night since we were..." She trailed off, that rosy flush of hers surging into a full-on blush. "But this place is kind of great."

Her bedroom was a half-story up from the main floor, as was the sitting area at the top of the stairs, where she still stood. I loved that part of the cabin. It was where I usually hung out and read during the quiet evenings here. Lounging on the old wooden futon or sitting on one of the two mismatched armchairs, curling my toes into the threadbare wool rug that really tied the room together. There was a built-in bookshelf along one wall up there too, full of books and games and puzzles. The puzzles were my favorite, and I'd done most of them by now. But I had my eye on the new one PeePaw must have added the last time he'd been up here.

"I know, right?" I said, not adding the *so why don't you hang around for a while?* that I wanted to. But this was probably one of those slow and steady wins the race situations. So I was gonna be slow, steady as a rock. "Are you hungry? I made coffee and bacon." I pointed my spatula toward the griddle where four pieces of egg-soaked bread were turning golden brown. "And French toast."

I loved to cook. And breakfast was my favorite meal to prepare. It was harder to show off my normal flair in this small, rustic kitchen. Without my setup and my spices and, most importantly, my sound system. But I had the Bluetooth speaker going, my "Old Cowboy Music" playlist warbling its charming twang in the background. I even picked up some fresh strawberries from the General yesterday. If I couldn't sway her with my charm, maybe I could do it with fruit, bacon, and maple syrup poured over melting butter. At the very least, she wouldn't leave on an empty stomach.

"I have to use the outhouse," she said, staring hungrily at the bacon already cooling beside the stove.

The memory of those hungry eyes staring up at me last night stirred the tiny hairs on the back of my neck. "You know"—I gave her a lazy grin—"having to use the outhouse doesn't actually preclude you from eating breakfast." Licking some butter from my fingertip, I said, "You can have it all, Hannah."

Her eyes twinkled, her lips parting like she wanted to say something. And as my brain whispered, "Come on, Hannah. Say it. Play with me," she walked down the stairs with Joey at her heels. When she reached the door, she stopped at the mat and stared at her shoes. The ones I'd lined up neatly next to mine.

"You found my other shoe?" She pointed to the mat. "And you... cleaned them?"

"Oh, yeah." I flipped the French toast over, because who was blushing now? That's right. Me. "I get up early, and when I took Joey out, I saw it poking up out of the mud." Not true. Not even remotely true. I searched for that motherfucker for ten minutes in the pissing rain before I finally found it. "And they weren't too messy." Also not true. Although both her shoes were filthy, the one that I'd rescued had been more mud than leather. "Cleaned right up."

I was watching the French toast, but she was watching me. Silently. Shit, maybe it was weird that I cleaned her shoes. Sometimes I went a little too hard on the choreplay.

Finally taking the umbrella down from its hook by the door, she said in a tone I could only describe as strictly professional, "Breakfast would be nice. Thank you." And then she walked out into the rain.

But hey. That could have gone a lot worse. We'd chatted. She'd smiled. She'd left her keys on the counter instead of grabbing them and running. All hope wasn't lost yet.

When she opened the door again, she shrieked as Joey raced inside between her legs, shaking rainwater all over her.

"Do you have a towel?" she asked, giving Joey a concerned frown as he curled up into a tight, shivering little bean on his chair by the woodstove. "He's all wet."

Placing two strips of bacon alongside two slices of French toast on her plate, I said, "I think there are some in the closet next to the stairs. Thank you."

While she pulled out a towel and gently dried off Joey's head and back, I told her, "I made coffee," instead of making some sort of blubbery sound at her being so sweet to my dog. "Do you want some?"

She moaned. "Yes, please."

Fuck. That moan. I'd heard that moan when my hand had been between her legs, when her nipple had been in my mouth. That moan was tattooed on my memory now.

My cock twitched behind my zipper, and I wrangled my thoughts as I pulled down a mug that said *Life Begins at* 80 from the shelf and filled it for her. But when she reached for it, I held the mug back.

"Not so fast," I said with a little *tut*. "I need to know how you take it."

"How I...take—" She closed her eyes for a long blink, then asked, "Do we have cream?"

"As a matter of fact, we do."

While she took her plate to the table, her eyelids fluttering when she inhaled the steam rising from the bacon, I opened the fridge.

"How does that work?" she asked when I pulled out the cream.

"Well," I replied, deadpan, "when whole milk is spun around at very high speeds, the fat separates, and cream can be skimmed off the top."

She blew out a laugh. "The refrigerator," she said, calling me out on my bullshit. "I thought we didn't have electricity out here."

"Oh, that." I popped the cream container open. "It's propane. Just like the lamps. Although, to be honest, I don't know how propane makes things cold." I shrugged. "Sorry to let you down."

"So disappointing." She sighed dramatically while pouring syrup over her French toast. "But I suppose your knowledge of the intricacies of modern dairy processing makes up for it."

Ah, she could give my bullshit right back to me. My weakness. We were gonna have some fun.

I poured the cream until she said when, then I set her coffee down next to her plate. Joining her at the table with my own plate and a carton of strawberries, I said, "I worked at a dairy farm for a summer when I was fifteen. I'll have you know that my dairy expertise is a deep and hard-earned source of pride."

She laughed again, so pretty. And I felt that same electric current zinging through the air between us, until she hit me with "If you can help me get my car unstuck, I'll leave this morning."

I didn't say anything at first, just picked a strawberry out of the carton and brought it to my lips. And when she asked, "Why are you looking at me like that?" I thought, *because I'm trying to figure out the perfect thing to say that will make you stay.*

But that would have been a dick move. I shouldn't try to manipulate her or this situation just because I didn't want her to leave. So I lowered the strawberry without taking a bite and said, "You should stay. I'll go."

"I don't want that. You got here first."

"It's a cabin, Hannah. Not a competition."

"I know." She cut into her French toast. "I still don't want to kick you and Joey out. And I should really get home."

There was something about that statement. Something so sad. And then I remembered what she'd said about her son. She'd come here to heal, to get away from her empty house. And I'd be damned if I sent her right back to it.

So I settled into my chair and crossed my arms over my chest, ready to plead my case that she stay and I go. Ready to make her realize that she could still get what she needed from this cabin, because I'd needed it once too, and I didn't want to take that from her.

But then she pointed her fork at me and said, "Don't do that."

"Do what?"

"You know what. You're either about to give me some deep insight into my current predicament, or you're going to sit there and wait silently until I offer one up. I'm a high school counselor, Darryn. I know the game." She twirled her fork in an all-encompassing circle. "I know *all* the games."

Ho, boy. She was onto me. I was gonna have to work a lot harder than I thought to keep her from leaving. Or maybe she'd see straight through all my tricks no matter how hard I tried. Maybe I just needed to be honest.

"Okay." Uncrossing my arms, I leaned forward to rest my elbows on the table. "Why do you want to leave? Would it be so terrible to stay here?" The unspoken end of that question—*with me?*—echoed like a shout across a canyon.

"I know your name," she said. "I know you're good at..." My brows shot to my hairline, until she added with a small laugh, "making coffee. But otherwise, I know nothing about you. And I don't routinely spend three-day weekends off the map with people I don't know."

Well, that was simple enough. "So let's not be strangers anymore." When I extended my hand across the table, she played along, shaking it once. Her grip was firm, but her skin was so soft. "Hi," I said. "I'm Darryn Madigan. I live in Olympia, Washington. I have three brothers—two older, one younger. I'm forty-nine years old. I work as an advocate for disabled vets, and I am a vet myself. I'm single—divorced. I also have a son, like you. But Jeremiah is twenty-eight. He lived in Olympia too, until he moved to Chicago four years ago for work." It still ached somewhere deep beneath my ribs when I thought about it, watching him drive away with a packed U-Haul, wondering if that was it. If that was the move that would end up being permanent. "That was actually when I started coming up here. I was trying to drive back home after visiting my brother who runs a sober living home in Red Falls, and I couldn't. I couldn't go back to Olympia knowing my kid wasn't there. So I pointed the car north and drove until I ended up at the General. Then I found a listing for PeePaw's pinned to the bulletin board."

"It's hard, right?" She leaned forward, eyes wide, like she was interested, maybe a little relieved. Like that moment when you're traveling in a foreign country and you hear someone speaking English and feel, almost immediately, understood. "It's hard when they leave."

"The hardest," I said sincerely. "But the cabin, the mountains, the silence up here... I don't know. It helped." *It could help you too, Hannah. Just give it a chance.* "Now, Joey and I come back here every year after I visit my big brother."

Her brows knitted together, and I could practically hear her talking herself out of staying. So I tossed Joey another piece of bacon, pinned her with a stare, and said, "Your turn," before she could.

Clearing her throat, she pulled her hair out of its knot and shook it loose. While I watched her dark waves fall over her shoulders, wishing I could run my fingers through them, she said, "I'm Hannah James. I also live in Washington, in Sequim."

I tried not to let my reaction to that information show, but Sequim was only a two-hour drive from Olympia. We were practically neighbors.

"I'm forty-six, also single, also divorced," she continued. "And, like I said, I'm a high school counselor."

"Which explains the student in the hallway freaking out about being pegged," I cut in.

She slapped a hand over her forehead. "I forgot I told you about that. I was such a mess."

"I didn't mind."

She met my stare, and I slid my foot forward until the tip of my toes touched hers. "I like your kind of mess."

She pulled her foot back.

Too much. Reel it in, D.

"What's that like," I asked, course correcting, "being a guidance counselor in this day and age?"

"Rough." She drew the word out, giving it at least two syllables. "Really rough. The pay is shit, the counselor to student ratios are ridiculous, the kids are really struggling right now, and at least half my day is spent on administrative tasks that have nothing to do with my actual job. If it wasn't for my work—" She froze, her eyes ballooning. Then she shot to her feet, the movement startling a bark out of Joey, and cried, "Holy shit! Steph!"

Reeling back, I asked, "Who's Steph?"

"My friend. My work wife." When she spotted her keys on the counter and snatched them up, I winced. Because those weren't going to do much for her at the moment.

"I was supposed to call her after I picked up my bag," she explained. "Steph was looking for another place for me to stay. But then I..."

"Got distracted?" I volunteered, not very helpfully if her exasperated expression was any indicator.

"I have to go." She slung her purse over her shoulder. "I have to get to the General. She's probably called in a missing persons by now."

Rising to my feet, I stepped into her space, took the keys from her hand, and set them back on the counter. "I already tried to get your car out this morning," I told her. "It wouldn't budge."

"You did? It wouldn't?"

"Hannah," I said, ready to lay it all on the line. "I'm not going to lie. I don't want you to leave. I think we could have a good time together." *Understatement.* "But the last thing I want is for you to feel stuck here. Whether you stay or go should be your choice. So I tried to free your car. Unfortunately, the mud didn't give a shit about what I wanted. But maybe we can try again later today."

Reaching for my mug, I drained the rest of my coffee. Then I swiped my keys from the counter and put hers back. "For now," I said while Joey scampered from his chair and sprinted toward the door, "I'll drive you to town. Hopefully I won't get stuck too."

CHAPTER SIX

HANNAH

His corded forearms tensed with every steering wheel jerk to keep us on the road. His jaw muscles flickered, his stare set with a determined focus through the rain-spattered windshield. And I was pretty much drooling in the passenger seat, watching the show he didn't realize he was putting on for me.

He was just so big. Mountain big. And in the daylight—without tears blurring my vision—I could see him more clearly. The little auburn curls brushing his neck, the silver strands along his temples, the tiny silver flecks in his stubble. And his eyes. So clear. So blue they looked impossible. An impossible color that was as impossible as this entire situation. I mean, where the hell did they even make men like Darryn Madigan? In a lab? Some underground factory whose sole purpose was to churn out ruggedly gorgeous sex gods?

And this morning, I nearly melted out of my clothes just talking to him, sitting across the table from him, fighting the urge to crawl into his lap, kiss those full lips and ask him to take me back to bed. It wasn't my fault. I mean, he cooked for me. He tried to free my car. He cleaned my fucking shoes.

"I can hear you thinking over there," he said, still staring straight ahead. "Worried about your friend?"

"Yes," I replied, then I narrowed my eyes. "But I'm also wondering if you're a real person."

His shoulders shook, and that was another thing. He was a chuckler. An easy laugher. A man whose smile lines were etched more deeply than the ones that came from frowning. In short: my personal kryptonite.

"Last I checked," he said. But when he turned his head, his eyes finding mine, my breath caught, and I turned away. There was something about the way he looked at me. Like he could see straight through me. Like I was cellophane, and he'd only have to pull a corner back and all my protective layers would unravel.

I was sure he could hear me thinking again, but when we pulled up to the General, he only hopped out, popped our umbrella, and ran around the front of his truck to open my door. Making sure the umbrella was covering my head, even at the expense of his, he took my hand, and we raced inside.

As soon as we burst through the door, my phone lit up with three missed calls and six missed texts. All from Steph. Nothing from William, though. Which was fine. It was good. He was off having fun, living his life, not thinking about me. Just like a normal kid.

Okay, fine, but would one text kill him?

"All good?" Darryn asked. When I showed him my phone, and all the notifications from Steph, he winced.

"I just need to call her back. Tell her I'm okay."

Smiling down at me, he tucked a stray strand of hair behind my ear. Then, as if realizing maybe he shouldn't have, he pulled his hand away quickly and wandered off to inspect the beer fridge.

"You *what?*" Steph shrieked after I gave her a brief and hushed rundown of the last sixteen hours.

Cupping my hand over the phone, even though he was probably too far away to hear, busy pulling out a six-pack of some bright yellow

IPA, I said, "I am so sorry I didn't get back to you last night. But that's why."

"Oh my god," she wheezed. "I mean, yeah, I was a little worried. But who the fuck cares? Hannah, you banged a hot stranger in a cabin in the woods. This is, like, the best possible scenario I could ever dream up for you. Was it good? Please tell me it was good."

Turning toward a shelf lined with colorful polished agate, I hid my blush in a beaded bracelet display and whispered, "Good doesn't even come close. I'll tell you all about it tomorrow. I'm heading home as soon as the rain stops, and we can get my car out—"

"What? Why?" she cut in, outraged, like I'd just told her I was going to throw out our office coffee maker and start drinking hot lemon water instead. "You have two more days up there."

Darryn moved to a bookshelf one row over, the six-pack tucked snuggly under his arm as he pulled out a copy of *The Field Guide to Montana Wildflowers*, flipped it over, and squinted at the back cover.

"Because," I started, then stalled out when he made an adorably thoughtful *huh* sound at something he'd read. "I mean, shouldn't I? Shouldn't I come home?"

"Fuck no," she insisted. "This is a grand slam. Or a slam dunk. It's some kind of sportsball-related slam. Wait, unless it's weird now. Is he being weird?"

"No," I said while realizing that maybe I was, watching him slide the wildflower book back into place, my mouth watering and skin tingling like it was a scene from a porn movie instead of a normal, everyday activity. "He's not being weird at all. He actually asked me to stay."

"Yes," she cheered. I was one hundred percent sure she'd just fist-pumped the air. "So stay with him. Stay with the hot guy who gave you great sex. My god."

"Yeah, but you know my track record with this kind of thing isn't great," I whispered again, slinking off toward the tourist hats. "You know I suck at casual sex. And I'm so emotionally vulnerable right now. It just seems like a really bad idea."

I'd done the whirlwind fling before. A few years ago. Until I caught feelings. He didn't. And it all blew up in my puffy, tear-soaked face.

"Okay," she said, shifting gears. "Then don't have sex with him again. Just make a new friend. With the world the way it is these days, we could all use more friends."

When she put it that way, it sounded perfectly reasonable to stay. Darryn and I were both seemingly nice people with at least a few things in common: a love of bacon, an appreciation for well-maintained outhouses, a fondness for making headboards thwack against walls... What harm could come from making a new friend? "You know what? You're right."

"Of course, I am," she said. "I'm always right. But send me a picture of his ID. Just in case. Okay, I gotta go. But I love you."

"Love you too."

Ending the call, I sent William a quick *Hope you're having a blast. Love you!* text. Then I joined Darryn at the bookshelf.

"Everything okay?" he asked.

"Steph wants me to send her a picture of your ID."

He didn't say a word, but his lips twitched when he pulled his wallet out of his back pocket and handed me his driver's license.

I snapped a pic of him looking phenomenal even at the DMV and sent it to Steph. Then I followed him to the counter.

"You want anything?" he asked right as Steph texted back: OH MY GOD HE'S A HEMSWORTH! and I locked my screen so fast I nearly broke a nail.

"Um, no," I said. "I'm good."

"A Hemsworth, huh?" *Busted.* "Tell your friend I'm flattered."

My phone buzzed again, and since I couldn't ignore it in case it was William texting me back, I took a peek. And so did Darryn.

"Wow," he said. "That's your work wife?"

Locking the screen again on the "Are you sure???" followed by a string of donut and eggplant emojis text from Steph, I said, "We might be getting a divorce."

"No way." He nudged my shoulder with his. "She's a keeper."

"Hey. You're still here," the cashier said as I shoved my phone back into my purse. "And, *ooh*." Their wide eyes swept over Darryn. "Was *this* who you were double-booked with?"

Darryn smirked at me.

My armpits started sweating. "Yep."

"That. Is. Amazing," they said. "Seriously. You might be my favorite Balsam Ridge magic couple ever."

"Magic, huh? Does this sort of thing happen a lot?" Darryn asked at the same time I insisted, "It's not like that."

The cashier gave me a *bless your heart* look, and coupled with Darryn's *oh, really?* expression, it was clear I was being called out. Because it was actually like that, per my request, as I'm sure Darryn recalled.

"It happens more than you might think," the cashier said. "We've had couples meet here, get married here, spend their anniversaries here. The magic is real."

Darryn's hand slid over my lower back, and he said, "Must be something in the air."

I choked on nothing.

"Are you staying for the rest of the weekend, then?" the cashier asked, their pierced eyebrow rising. "Together?"

"Hmm." Removing his hand, Darryn turned toward me. "I don't know. Are we?"

My heart thumped, and I reminded myself that we would just be friends. Just two new friends enjoying some peace and quiet. I almost believed it too.

Lost for a second in his clear blue eyes, I blinked, then handed him his license back. While he took it from me with a brush of his fingertips over mine, I said, "I think so."

His smile was incandescent.

"But"—I spun around, walked to the back of the store, and returned with a bottle of red—"If I'm staying, I'm going to need this."

* ⋆ ⋆ · ⋆

WHEN WE MADE our way back into the cabin, Joey leaped down from his chair and ran straight to me. "I should unpack my car," I said, picking Joey up and nuzzling his soft little cheek. "There's a bag in the trunk that Steph packed for me. I don't even know what's in there."

After shaking out our umbrella, Darryn rounded the counter, set my bottle of wine down, and pulled a corkscrew out of a drawer.

"Are we starting early?" I asked while an unfamiliar spark flared in my chest. If I had to give it a name, I'd call it giddiness.

"Why not?" he said. "I checked the weather when we were at the General. It's going to rain all day. We're stuck inside. Nowhere to go. Nothing to do." He twisted the corkscrew, his forearm muscles straining, then he pulled the cork free with a promising *pop*. "Come on, Hannah." He winked at me. "Let's be irresponsible."

I licked my lips, and he stared at them. While he poured the wine, he still stared at them. I'd never been so acutely aware of my mouth before.

"Here," he said as he passed me the glass. Then he snatched my keys from the counter. "Relax. Enjoy your wine." He winked. "And I'll go find out what you've got in your trunk."

A few minutes later, his big shoulders pushed through the door, and he stomped back into the cabin with rain-damp curls and the bag Steph had packed for me in his hand.

"Here you go," he said, placing the bag on the kitchen counter. And while he reached into the fridge for a beer, I unzipped it.

I saw my running shoes first, nestled between a power bank, a headlamp, and an absolutely gigantic box of condoms.

"Wow." He grinned at my literal lifetime supply of latex. "Your friend must have heard about the Balsam Ridge magic too."

I closed my eyes. Steph was going to get an earful. "I don't... It's not... I'm not usually—"

"On the prowl for a hookup?" His lips tilted, touching the rim of his bottle before he took a sip.

"Definitely not," I reiterated. Because like I'd told Steph, I sucked at casual sex. I was so bad at it, in fact, that while I pulled the shoes and headlamp and condoms out of the bag, followed by a water purifier, fire starters, body wipes, bug spray, sunscreen, and a first aid kit, as well as a boatload of nonperishable food, jealousy compelled me to ask, "But were you? On the prowl?"

He set down his beer with a dull *clank*, his expression sobering. "Do you want the truth?"

My stomach clenched into a tight, anxious knot. And that tight knot was exactly my problem. That was why I didn't do casual. It wasn't that I confused sex with love or expected some weird kind of loyalty after I slept with someone. My brain was in touch with reality. For instance, my brain knew that we were two fully grown adults who'd had a consensual hookup and didn't owe each other anything. It was my body that refused to get the memo.

My body reacted to intimacy like it was important and meaningful and anything but casual. It used to make me feel like there was something wrong with me, like I was missing whatever gene allowed everyone else to separate the physical from the emotional. As I got older, I was finally able to accept that it wasn't a bad thing. It was just how I functioned. Even if my frazzled emotional state had forgotten all about that little fact yesterday.

But today was a new day. A fresh start. Today, we were only two people sharing a cabin. So I nodded with a practiced nonchalance and replied, "Sure."

Placing his hands on his hips, which emphasized the way his jeans sat low beneath the hem of his T-shirt, he explained, "I'm a single, middle-aged man who sometimes feels the clock ticking on his love life. So I'm always looking. I'm always hopeful." His head cocked toward his bedroom door. "It's why I have condoms, in case you were wondering. I mean." He raised an amused brow at my stockpile of prophylactics. "I don't have as many as *you* do, but..."

"Ha ha," I muttered while my face went so hot it could melt a polar ice cap.

"But I have never had sex with a stranger," he said, his voice leveling off like this was important to him. Like it was meaningful. "Not until you."

Oh no, I thought as my body reacted again, leaning toward him all on its own as he reached out for me.

He caressed my cheek, brushed his thumb over my lower lip, and said, "Doubt I ever will again, either. Since I hit perfection on my first try."

My immediate instinct was to roll my eyes, but his were so steady, so unflinching, that I wondered if he meant it. I wondered if I'd met the world's last earnest man. And then I wondered what it might have been like if I'd met him under different circumstances. If he lived in my town or if I lived in his. If the first time I saw those crystal-clear blue eyes was at the coffee shop on my corner. If I'd stood in line behind him, admiring the broad expanse of his shoulders, shivering when the vibrations of his deep voice skittered over my skin while he made charming small talk with the barista. And when he turned around, he'd notice me, and his eyes would sparkle in the morning sunlight streaming through the windows. And I'd be lost. Tongue tied. Probably forget my order. Maybe even my name. Maybe, if things had been different, we could have become something more than casual.

With one last brush of his thumb, tugging down just enough to part my lips, he dropped his hand and spun my bag around. And while I told my pounding heart and heated blood to get a grip, he started unpacking my food.

He lined up my tuna and crackers and oatmeal in tidy rows beneath the cupboards, and I pressed my fingers over the ghost of his thumbprint on my lip. He shook the half-ton box of condoms before putting them back in my bag, and I melted at the note of hope in his expression. He placed my running shoes next to his by the door, and I could feel my eyes turning into little hearts. And that was when it hit me, like a bowling ball hurled into my chest at lightspeed. It wasn't just my body. My brain was invested now too. Because I liked him. I liked Darryn Madigan.

I liked him enough, that under normal circumstances, I might have risked spending the rest of the weekend indulging in him. But these weren't normal circumstances. This wasn't a flingable weekend for me. I didn't have the luxury of convincing my heart that it wouldn't be hurt or broken after it was over and I never saw him again. Because my heart was already broken, and the whole purpose of this weekend was to focus on putting it back together. I owed myself that much at least.

So after thanking him for unpacking my trunk, I took my glass of wine, pulled the cozy mystery I'd brought with me out of my carry-on, and curled up in one of the armchairs on the second floor.

I tried to be good. I tried to focus. But instead of reading my book, I watched him over the pages. I watched him clean the pan from breakfast, rinse our coffee mugs, and wipe down the counter in broad, muscle-rippling strokes. I watched him retreat to his room, and I tried not to imagine what he could be doing in there that made all those bumping and jostling noises. Changing clothes? Doing pushups? Touching himself while thinking of me?

It wasn't until later in the day, when he took Joey out, that I finally managed to read a full page. But when he returned and bent over to dry Joey's little paws, his back turned toward me his butt just right there for me to stare at, I gave up.

"How's your book?" he asked with perfect comic timing.

"Great," I lied while Joey trotted up the stairs and curled up on the futon next to me. "Can't put it down."

"I've noticed." It was a disappointed grumble, like he'd been waiting for me to forget about the book and remember him instead.

While my skin tingled from Darryn's grumble, Joey trembled from the cold. Pulling a blanket from the back of the couch, I tucked it in around him, nice and tight.

"Aw, that's sweet," Darryn said, and I decided that his shoulders and chest in his soft, zip-up hoodie should have been illegal. Especially when he added, "I'm cold too. Can I be next?"

"How old is Joey?" I asked instead of answering. Because he was joking, obviously.

"Not sure." Crossing to the kitchen, he took a plate down from the cupboard. "Vet thinks around five."

"Is he a rescue?"

"Yep," he said. "I was lonely after Jeremiah, my kid, moved away. So I went to the shelter kind of on a whim. I didn't know if I wanted a dog or a cat or a turtle. I wasn't entirely sure I wanted anything. But I took one step inside, and there Joey was, staring up at me through the bars of his cage, panting and wagging his tail like he was so happy I finally showed up. Like he'd been waiting. And I thought, *I guess I'm getting a dog today*. Because that's him. That's my guy."

"He's adorable." Every cell inside my body swooned at the image of Darryn and Joey meeting for the first time.

But then Darryn said, "He's my best bud," and the weight of the word pressed on my heart.

I missed *my* bud. I missed William. My eyes stung, my voice thick when I said, "That's really sweet."

Like he was reading my mind, Darryn opened the fridge and asked the contents inside, "Did you get in touch with your son at the General?"

I rubbed at the William-shaped ache beneath my sternum. "I texted him, but he didn't text back while we were there. He's having fun, so it makes sense. What eighteen-year-old thinks about checking in with their mom when they're at the beach with their friends?"

As he pulled out salami, a triangle of pale cheese, and a carton of blueberries and set them on the counter, he asked, "What's he going to school for?"

"Environmental law. UCLA."

"Really?" He opened my box of crackers, and my stomach rumbled when he started putting together a girl-dinner snack plate. "That's amazing."

"He's the coolest kid." Pride swelled in me the way it always did when I talked about my son. "My ex and I got divorced when he was eight. And even before then, his dad was usually gone for work or... other things." Things like having multiple affairs all over the pacific northwest. "So it's mostly just been us. Just me and William."

"You two are pretty tight then, huh?" he asked while fanning out circular slices of salami on the plate.

"We are. It's funny too, because I was terrified when I got pregnant. I didn't know if I'd be a good mom. I didn't have the best role model, and I honestly thought I'd suck at it."

"Not possible," he said as he placed cheese slices next to the salami. "You've got *good mom* written all over you."

I swayed a little in my chair, not realizing until that moment that a compliment could make a person feel lightheaded.

"But I was in my early twenties and scared shitless when J was born," he added. "So I get it."

"We hadn't been trying," I explained. "I didn't even think I wanted kids. And our marriage was already rocky. But then William arrived, and everything changed so fast it was like a dividing line in my life. Like there was a who I was before him, and a who I am after, and they're totally different people."

His head bobbed while he poured some blueberries onto the middle of the plate. "I know the feeling."

After taking a sip of my wine, I said, "One thing they don't tell you about parenting is how amazing it is to watch this person, this little soul, become an adult. You have this baby, this blank slate, and you look at them like, 'Who are you?' Because you have no idea. And then they grow up and turn into this kind, funny, and talented adult with a completely unique way of moving through the world. They're a little like you, a little like their dad, but mostly they're just themselves. A whole, brand-new person. And you get to witness it happen in complete and total…"

"Awe," he said, finding the word I'd been searching for. Like he knew. Like he'd felt it too.

"Yeah."

Climbing the half staircase in two big steps, he set the snack plate on the coffee table, gave Joey a head scratch, and then took the chair beside me. "Do you want to talk about it?" he asked carefully.

"About my brand-new status as an empty nester?"

He placed a slice of salami onto a cracker, topped it with a hunk of cheese, and handed it to me. "I'm a good listener."

"Thanks." I took a bite, and my eyes flared. "Oh my god," I moaned at the sharp and salty explosion of flavor in my mouth. "This cheese. It's amazing. Where'd you get it?"

After swallowing his own cracker snack, he said, "It's from the dairy farm. The one where I used to work. They have a booth at our farmers' market, and I never miss a Saturday." He lowered his voice. "Mary still gives me the staff discount. But that is highly confidential information. You can't tell a soul; I'm not kidding."

"I would never," I said, aghast that he'd even imply it. Or at least pretending to be. "A scandal like that could rock the entire artisanal cheese community."

"It could rock the Madigan family game night, that's for sure. If my mother ever found out about the deals Mary gives me, I'd be power washing my parents' deck until the cows come home. Literally."

I tamped down my smile, which felt embarrassingly bright. "Do your parents live in Olympia too?"

"We all do. My parents. My brothers. All except for Madigan."

"Wait," I said, baffled. "You have a brother named Madigan? Madigan Madigan?"

He shook his head, eyes sparkling again. "No. My oldest brother's name is Matthew. But everyone aside from his family calls him Madigan."

When I cut him a sideways glance, he said, "Yeah, I know. The fact that he got the nickname just because he's the oldest is total bullshit. And then he got famous and claimed the nickname on an international scale, and the rest of us knew we didn't stand a chance. I usually call him Mattie, but I visited him in Red Falls right before I came up here. The nickname always sneaks back in after a few days of hearing everyone around me use it."

"Matthew Madigan," I repeated. "That name does sound familiar."

"He played lead guitar for the Makers. The '90s grunge band. You know 'em?"

I grinned. "Of course I do. Jeez, Darryn, you've got a famous brother, a secret cheese connection, *and* you're phenomenal in bed? You're, like, the total package."

Record scratch. Did I just say that? I looked down at my glass, because what the hell was in this wine?

It took close to an eternity for me to look back up at him, but when I did, the mischievous glint in his eyes pulled my skin tight, and I blurted out, "We used to have game night too," before he could say anything that might have made me crawl into his lap. "And when William got older, his friends would join us. It was my favorite night of the week."

His expression flattened, except for that glint. It was still there when he said, "And now you're going to miss it."

It wasn't a question, so I didn't give him an answer. I wasn't sure I could have anyway. Not around the sharp lump lodging itself in my throat. Because, yes, I was going to miss it. Like a lost limb.

While my eyes burned, Darryn's hand slid over my knee. "This," he said, giving my knee a squeeze, "your kid going to college, leaving home, it's a big deal. It's another dividing line in your life. It's a top ten-er."

"A top ten-er?" I asked.

"It's something my dad always says." He pulled his hand away. "A top ten moment. It's like when you look back at all the things that shaped you, that made your life what it was, William going away to college will be in the top ten. So it makes sense that it feels huge. Top ten-ers are supposed to feel huge."

I studied the wine in my glass, feeling the truth of the statement settle over me—also still feeling the warmth of his palm through my leggings.

While he pushed himself up to his feet to peruse the bookshelf, I said, "Sometimes I wish I could just zoom out, you know? Just wave my hand and see the big picture. See his life in five years, ten, and know that he'll be fine, and that I'll be fine, and that this is just the way things go. Because being so close to it now, it's hard to see past this moment. This great big goodbye."

"Oh, yeah. I like that." He pulled out a sci-fi book, then pushed it back in. "Life definitely needs a zoom feature. Instant perspective." When he squatted to check out the puzzles and games on the lowest shelf, his jeans stretching tight over his thick thighs, he said, "You're a very insightful person, Hannah. I bet it helps you in your job."

He'd already given me more compliments than I'd received in the last calendar year, and it was doing something dangerous to me. My heart was beating too fast, too hard, and all my senses were heightened: smell, sound, touch. A gust of wind at that moment would have felt like a hurricane.

"And as someone who has already lived through the great big goodbye *twice*," he said, still squatting, "do you want some good news?"

"There's good news?" I asked as my shoulders finally started to distance themselves from my ears.

"Depends on your perspective, I guess. But in this economy, he'll probably have to move back in with you in four years anyway."

I groaned. "These poor kids."

"I know, right? But would you mind?" he asked over his shoulder. "If he did?"

"No." Emphasizing the point with a head shake, I said, "His bedroom will always be waiting for him. I promised him I'd never turn it into a home gym or rent it out. It's his for as long as he wants or needs it."

"That's what I told J too, that there would always be a safe place for him at our house, no matter what. And he's taken advantage of it several times. It's a massive change the first time they leave, but it's not goodbye. I promise."

We were silent as he pulled out a one-thousand-piece puzzle of wolves howling at the moon that was still in the wrapper. Then I said, "You're pretty insightful too."

His lips hitched, his eyes crinkling at the corners, and I wanted to add, "You're also just pretty." So pretty that my fingertips ached to trace those crinkling lines, my lips ached to press feather-soft kisses along his cheekbones. So pretty that I couldn't look away from him or help but notice that he wasn't looking away from me. Then he made a show of shivering.

"It's getting chilly in here again. Should I start another fire?" His brow ticked. "Warm things up?"

Sense memories tumbled through me. Fingers sifting through my hair, grasping my knee, hiking my leg up. "A fire—" I cleared the wobble from my voice and tried again. "A fire would be good."

"Mm-hmm," he murmured, still staring, and I was cellophane again, my desire for him on full display. "Then I'll get right on it."

He built and tended to the fire, then he sat at the table, opened his puzzle, and I pretended to read my book again. After a while, the fire turned the cabin nice and warm. Or maybe it was him, the way he searched for puzzle pieces, furrowing his brow and chewing on his lower lip. The way he started singing along with his playlist, his voice deep and quiet and soulful. Either way, I was suddenly so hot I had to whip off my hoodie.

Fighting to regain a shred of the composure I'd built my adult life around, I sat and read while I sipped the wine he refilled my glass with, nibbled on the snacks he kept bringing me—sliced apples, four squares of a chocolate bar, a bowl of the most delicious dark red cherries I'd ever tasted—and finally started to let cabin life sink into me. I finally started to breathe.

But sitting and breathing was a skill. One I hadn't honed. And as afternoon settled in, I did the opposite, shifting my position over and over until Darryn said, "Antsy?"

His eyes were glued to his puzzle, but I felt his attention on me like a spotlight in the dark, tracking my movements while I stood and started pacing above him.

"Yeah." I reached my hands toward the ceiling and arched my back, needing to stretch after sitting for so long. The motion pulled my top up, exposing a sliver of my stomach to the warm air inside the cabin.

When I lowered my arms and turned his way, I found him staring at me, at my body.

"It's easy to get bored on days like this," he said absently, lazily, his eyes finally rising from my belly and breasts until they met mine. "Easy to get antsy."

Under his watchful attention, my clothes felt too tight, itchy. Tugging my top back down, I said, "I guess we'll just need to find something to do."

I'd only meant that maybe we could play a game, like Scrabble or cribbage, but he turned back to his puzzle, notched a piece into place, and suggested, "We could mess around."

My heart screeched to a halt. It took three solid seconds for me to remember what words were. And no sooner had I found them than he made direct, unflinching eye contact with me and said, "I'd love to make you come again."

My throat spasmed. My knees nearly gave way. This offer, this ache in my bones to take him up on it, this was not part of my no more sex plan.

"Darryn," I started to say while he pushed himself up from the table, making my breath stall out somewhere in my lungs, "I'm not sure"—he climbed the stairs, prowling toward me—"it's a good idea"—

he moved into my space, and heat radiated from his bonfire of a body—
"to turn this"—he reached for me, cradled my face, and when he licked
his lips, I squeezed my eyes shut and blurted out, "into a fuck cabin."

Silence slammed down between us like an anvil dropped from an
airplane. Until he lowered his hands and asked, "Did you just say,
'fuck cabin'?"

"What?" Blood shot into my cheeks. "It's a thing. Strangers stuck
in the woods, miles from civilization, nothing to do but—"

"Fuck?" he suggested, his pupils big and round and black as
night.

I nodded slowly while he stepped even closer.

"And that would be a bad thing?" he asked, brushing my hair off
my right shoulder. And then my left. "Letting me fuck you? Letting
me make you feel good?"

My fingers curled around his hips and held on. For balance, probably. And why was letting him make me feel good a bad thing? Why
did I not want to let this man fuck me until I couldn't move? *Come
on, brain. You have one job.*

It was important to explain myself, obviously. But with him
standing so close to me, touching me, the only words pinging around
my mind were *yes* and *now* and *more*. I needed a different tactic.
Like, what would I tell my students in this situation? What would I
tell William? As long as it was consensual and safe, let 'er rip?

Jesus, no.

I would tell them to be careful. I'd tell them that it's important to
know their own boundaries and reactions when it came to intimacy,
and, more importantly, to respect them. And that no matter what,
clear communication about any fears or concerns or expectations was
nonnegotiable.

That's what I'd tell them. And it's what I needed to tell myself.

"It wouldn't be bad," I answered, a little breathless because he'd
slid his hand beneath my hair and had started massaging my neck.
"Or it would, but only because I'd like it."

His hand stilled. "Isn't that kind of the point?"

I huffed a laugh, then my eyelids sank as he started massaging again. "I meant that I'd like it too much. You met me at a weird time—oh god, that's good," I rasped while he squeezed. "But, normally, I'm really not cool and casual about sex. I get attached too easily, even if I don't mean to. I know that's probably not what you want to hear. I know you probably wanted a hot weekend in a—"

"Fuck cabin?" he filled in for me, rubbing a particularly sore muscle so firmly with his thumb I left my body for a second.

"Right," I breathed, grasping his hips more tightly as I swayed on my feet. "But with everything going on in my life right now, I can't afford to get attached. I'm already an emotional wreck, and one great big goodbye was enough for me this week. I don't think I could handle another one. I'm really sorry."

I didn't love the way that admission felt. Especially when he pulled his hand away from my neck. But I talked a lot of talk at work, always presenting myself as a grounded, stable surface my students could cling to when their worlds were falling apart. Always showing up day after day with unfailing self-regulation and calm, rational reactions—even if I cried privately in the staff bathroom from time to time. And it felt good knowing that when the chips were down, even when those chips were massaging my neck like I'd paid for it, I could walk the walk too.

Gazing down at me, Darryn brushed my bangs back with a soft swipe of his fingers, then he gave my forehead a kiss so sweet it made my chin wobble. "You have nothing to be sorry about," he said. "Nothing at all. I am not here with you because I want a hot weekend. I mean, if you change your mind, definitely let me know."

Laughing, I loosened my hold on his hips.

"But I'm happy hanging out with you. I'm happy just being here with you." His chest rose and fell through a big sigh. "And you're probably right. More sex might blow up in both our faces. Because you're not the only person who'd like it too much."

Taking a step back, and about five degrees of warmth with him, he shook himself out and said, "So we'll be good. We'll behave. No messing around." Holding up his hand, he pressed his thumb over his pinky. "Scout's honor."

"You were a boy scout?" I asked.

"Not even close," he answered, and after we both laughed at the break in tension, he said, "I'm antsy too, though. Gotta get this restless energy out somehow." With a wry smile, he tilted his head toward the door. "Wanna go for a run?"

CHAPTER SEVEN

DARREN

AFTER AN HOUR of self-imposed agony while I stared at her ass in her leggings—because I was the genius who'd decided to run behind her down a trail through the woods, winding around trees and pounding through puddles—we stumbled back down PeePaw's driveway, panting and worked and completely soaked. Our shoes were covered in mud, our shirts plastered to our skin, and fuck, it felt good.

Endorphins raced through my bloodstream as we caught our breaths on the porch, smiling at each other, at our drenched clothes and wet hair.

"I needed that," she said, bending over, resting her hands on her knees.

"Me too." When she looked up at me, I fought every urge to sweep the strand of damp hair clinging to her cheek free.

Her gaze trailed from my lips to my chin, down my throat, hovering there for a moment. Then she stood and squeezed the rain out of her ponytail. "I guess we'd better get dry."

I nodded. And after we grabbed our towels, she went to her room, I went to mine, and we reconvened near the woodstove a few minutes later, freshly body-wiped clean. I'd changed into my favorite navy joggers and a white T-shirt. But Hannah, *oh, Hannah...*

A soft pink camisole skimmed over her breasts and down her belly, both partially obscured by the oversized, cable-knit cardigan hanging loosely from her shoulders. The look was sensational, but the real star of the show was the matching pair of fluttery shorts I just knew would come off easily with one small tug.

Fuck.

"Sorry." Probably noticing me staring at her with my jaw on the floor, she wrapped her sweater tightly around herself. "I'm still a little hot after the run, and these were the only pajamas I packed that weren't warm. But if they're too, um, revealing, I can go change."

"It's fine. No problem," I said, even though those shorts were *definitely* a problem. "You can walk around naked as long as you're comfortable, and I will still behave." My own brain cackled at me, hysterically. "Are you hungry?" I asked, my brain getting a kick out of that one too.

"Starving," she replied. And was she staring at my mouth? My shoulders? Were sparks literally flying between us?

Fuck, fuck, fuck.

"Good." In case she was checking me out, I crossed my arms in front of my chest and flexed. "I'll make dinner."

"Or I can," she said, attention locked on my pecs. "You've cooked everything so far. I'm happy to do my share."

Stepping close enough to smell the rain in her still-damp hair, I said, "Yeah, but I love to cook. And I love watching you get to relax. It's a win-win for me, really."

Her throat bobbed through a swallow that seemed to bend time, her eyes big and round when she said, "Okay. Um, thank you."

I reached out for her, straightening the collar of her sweater where it had curled under. And maybe I shouldn't have done that. I definitely shouldn't have let my knuckles brush along her collarbone the way I did. But even though I was taking her cue on not getting physical—or trying to—I never said I'd stop flirting with her. Because while she merely thought she liked me too much, I already knew I liked her too much. And maybe that should scare me the same way it seemed to scare her. But it didn't. Besides, flirting was basically my mother tongue.

I walked past her into the kitchen, and she stood in place for several seconds before heading back up the stairs. While I watched her go, I tortured myself with mental images of how good her ass must look in those shorts under her cardigan. Until she glanced back over her shoulder and caught me staring.

"Sorry," I said sheepishly. "My bad."

She rolled her eyes at me, but it was playful, not annoyed. And while she sat in her chair and turned her attention back to her book, I boiled water for pasta, caramelized some shallots, then added garlic, peas, and prosciutto to the pan. While the pasta cooked, I thought she might have actually read instead of just pretending to like she'd been doing all day. Hard to read a book when you never turn the page.

Ten minutes later, noodles cooked, wine poured, and dinner carefully plated, I called her down.

With her sweater wrapped tightly around her waist again, hiding everything but her phenomenal legs, she followed Joey down the stairs and took the seat across from me. And it felt so good, so right. Preparing food for her, sitting at the table with her, watching her fork travel from her plate to her lips. When she took her first bite of pasta, when she made a sound so indecent it scrambled my brain, that felt right too.

"Where did you learn to cook like this?" she asked while I shifted in my seat.

"My mom." I pierced some penne with my fork. "Laurie Madigan is an amazing cook. Her lasagna is legendary. I'm the second youngest, and with three other brothers constantly vying for her attention, I learned at a pretty young age that if I offered to help cook, not only did I get out of cleanup, but I also scored lots of quality time with her."

"Darryn, are you a mama's boy?" Her eyes lit up. Like she already knew the answer and it delighted her.

"And damn proud of it," I said, smiling right back. "I talk to her every day. The only time I didn't was when I was deployed and couldn't. I texted her while we were in the General this morning. Mattie got mixed up with drugs when we were kids and battled addiction for years. That's why he runs the sober living home now. But during his really bad years, when I was just a teenager, I barely left Mom's side."

A divot dove between her brows. "I'm so sorry. I've had lots of students with substance abuse issues in their families. It can be really hard on everyone. And when it's a sibling, the other kids often carry the silent weight of supporting their parents."

"It was hard on all of us, for sure," I agreed, and I loved this little glimpse of how she must be at work. Compassionate, caring, knowledgeable without being condescending. Her students must adore her. "And maybe I did carry some weight, but that's only because it wasn't just hard for Mom. It was impossible. She had to watch Mattie change, see him high as shit on MTV interviews after the band blew up, read about him wrecking hotel rooms and getting arrested. And she couldn't do anything to help him. My dad kind of shut down after a while, but my mom never gave up. She never let herself feel a moment's peace until Mattie finally came through the other side. Which took a really long time." I bit my cheek at the memories, the sleepless nights, the tears, my anger. "Anyway, it solidified my role in the family as Mom's shield. Which my other two brothers teased me about mercilessly, of course. Not Mattie, though. He's only ever been grateful that I was there for her."

"I'm not really close with my mom," she said, poking at her pasta. "She was a single parent and worked long hours, and I was a very self-sufficient kid. I think she never really wanted to be a parent, and I was too easily convinced that I didn't need her to be one. I love her, don't get me wrong. But we've always been more like acquaintances, I guess. I don't really know what's going on in her life, and she doesn't know what's going on in mine. We talk a couple times a year. She sends William birthday cards. Sometimes we'll visit her for Christmas or Thanksgiving, but she prefers to go on trips with her friends over the holidays. So it's not very often."

"Was that hard for you growing up?" I asked. "Not being close? Being on your own like that?" Because it sounded hard. To this mama's boy, it sounded hard and lonely and scary.

"Sometimes." She set down her fork. "Like, I knew she'd be there to make sure I got to school on time or to take me to the doctor if I was sick. But she didn't take care of me, if that makes sense. She didn't tuck me in at night or read me bedtime stories. She didn't help brush the tangles from my hair or talk to me about boys."

"She never made you laugh until you cried during a tickle fight?" I suggested. And I didn't reach out to take her hand, but I wanted to.

"Is that something girls do with their moms?" she asked. "Have tickle fights?"

"Girls?" I scoffed. "Please. Jeremiah and I *still* have tickle fights when he comes home to visit."

"I can honestly say that I have never been in a tickle fight." She sighed. "And now I really feel like I've missed out."

"Look, Hannah. If you need to have a tickle fight, I'll take you down to the floor right now. I don't give a fuck."

A laugh rocketed out of her, and her smile, blindingly bright, *that* was the one. The one that would have taken me to my knees if I hadn't already been sitting. Fuck, she was so beautiful. Maybe she'd just let me kiss her. We could just make out for the next day and a half. We wouldn't have to go any farther than that. But even as the thought crossed my mind, the thought of her lips and the softness of her mouth, my joggers started feeling too tight. Kissing her would never be enough.

"When I had William," she said while I tried to get myself in check, "that was one thing that really mattered to me, that we were close. I never wanted him to wonder how important he was to me. I wanted him to know that no matter what, he was my number one.

Especially since his father, my cheating piece-of-shit ex," she said with open disdain, "only ever put himself first. And I don't expect it at all, but if William ended up texting me every day, talking to me every day, I'd be the happiest mom on the planet. So it's nice that you do that for yours." Her left brow rose. "Even if you are keeping fancy cheese secrets from her."

Snorting, I raised my beer and tilted it toward her. "To mama's boys," I said, "and to the mamas who inspire them."

She touched the rim of her wine glass to the lip of my bottle, and then we drank and ate and talked a bit more. When we were both finished with dinner, she insisted on doing the dishes.

Sitting back in my chair, I sipped my beer as she poured one of the bottles I'd filled with well water this morning into the sink, lathered up a sponge, and started scrubbing our plates. I tried not to stare, tried to be respectful, but when she peeled off her cardigan after her sleeves wouldn't stay pushed up, I lost the fight.

She'd tied her hair up into a knot, and her long, graceful neck, her hands and arms all wet and sudsy, her breasts in that tank top and her ass in those shorts—which filled them out better than I'd even imagined—kicked my mind straight into the gutter.

I needed something to do. I needed a distraction. I needed to focus my brain on something besides objectifying this woman. So I pulled over my half-finished puzzle from the far side of the table and bent my head to my task. Find pieces, place pieces, make a pretty wolf picture. I could do this.

But when she swiped the back of her hand across her forehead, my puzzle pieces blurred in front of me. When she reached up to put a plate away in the tall cupboard, exposing the smooth skin of her lower back, my hands balled into fists. When she leaned over to wipe the countertop down, her top falling open just enough to show me a sinful line of cleavage, my cock stirred to life.

Focus. Puzzle. Pieces. Pretty picture.

Taking mercy on me, she wrapped herself back up in her sweater before joining me at the table and asking, "Can I help?"

"Of course," I said, then muttered, "I can use all the help I can get," while hoping my inappropriately half-hard dick wasn't as obvious as it felt.

Spreading pieces out on the table in front of her, straightening them into tidy lines with her slender fingers, she asked, "How long have you been working with vets?"

Ooh, was this the let's-get-to-know-each-other-better portion of the weekend? If so, I was all in.

"Let's see." I ran my knuckles over my cheek stubble. "I came home from my last tour in 2006, then I spent a few years falling apart and fighting to get my shit back together." Finding a piece of the moon, I clicked it into place. "So probably around 2010. I think that's when things started turning around for me, and I decided I wanted to give back."

"Were you in Iraq?"

"Afghanistan," I said. "Two deployments. And the second one was..." I blew out a breath, because remembering to breathe was important when I talked about that time. "It was bad. I lost a lot of friends."

She reached for my hand, her fingers wrapping around mine as she said, sincerely, "I'm sorry, Darryn."

Still looking at my hand even after she pulled hers away, I said, "Thank you. But I'm okay. I have lots of support. And working to make sure other vets have the support they need probably helps me the most. It's weird how that happens."

"Not weird at all," she said. "It's the helper-therapy principal."

I hadn't heard of that before, so I asked, "What's that?"

"It's this theory that when someone helps someone else, the benefits aren't one-sided. Like, the act of helping itself can give us a sense of well-being and connection with others." She picked up a piece, put it back down, and met my stare. "So you help vets, and your brother helps addicts. Maybe caregiving runs in your family."

"Not for everyone," I said with a laugh. "My other two brothers are a lawyer and an investment banker. They both think Mattie and I are ridiculous idealists who"—I drew air quotes—"don't understand how the world works. If I never hear the words financial responsibility again, it'll be too soon."

"Oh, what do they know." She flipped her wrist through the air. "Money isn't everything."

"Exactly. Like, who needs three houses?"

"Or a boat?" she added.

"Or trucks that were made in this century?" I said.

"Or to pay off their student loans?" she tacked on.

"Or to ever be able to retire?"

She laughed. "Maybe some of us *want* to work until we're dead. Not everyone longs for the days when they can finally learn woodworking or get really serious about their bowling game, Madigan brothers."

I raised my beer to my grinning lips—something I'd started doing a bit more deliberately, because she always watched me—and after taking a sip, I asked, "Why did you get into counseling high schoolers?"

When she suggested flatly, "Because I hate myself?" I cracked up.

"I'm kidding," she said. "I actually love my job. It's hard most of the time. Thankless almost all the time. But every once in a while, I get to help a kid. That's why I got into it. I had an amazing counselor when I was in high school. They made me feel like I wasn't so alone." Finding another piece of the moon, she clicked it into place. "I guess I wanted to pass it on. Even if I never realized I'd spend so much time dealing with adolescent relationship disasters."

"Ah, yes," I said. "The dark side of the helper-therapy principle. We don't always get to decide what we're helping with or whether it will or won't involve pegging."

"We definitely do not," she said with a smile, and then we lapsed into a comfortable silence, working the puzzle together while the rain pattered against the roof.

After finding homes for a few more pieces, she took a break to visit the outhouse, letting Joey out too. When she came back in, she walked up the stairs with Joey at her heels and disappeared into her room. I couldn't make out the things she was saying to my dog in there, but just hearing her talk to him, hearing his claws clack excitedly over the wood floor, sent a sweet pang through my chest. Maybe it wasn't just me. Maybe Joey had been lonely lately too.

Eventually, she came back out, having traded her shorts for somehow even sexier wide-leg lounge pants. She paused at the top of the stairs, turned to study the bookshelf with her hands on her hips, and...I don't know. I liked it. I liked watching her walk around the cabin. I liked sharing the same space with her. Sharing the same moment. I liked imagining that we'd done it for years, and it was way too easy to imagine doing it even longer.

I could already see her in my house, coming home at the end of a long day, dropping her bag on the little table by the door and rubbing her neck. Maybe I'd open my arms to her, and she'd come to me. Maybe she'd run her fingers over my stubble as I asked how her day was. Maybe I'd kiss her forehead, run her a bath, make her dinner. Make love to her until we both fell asleep, cuddled up and happy.

And, yeah, shit, she definitely had a point about not getting physical again. My head wasn't right around her. She had a hold of me, and if she ever let me get a hold of her too, I'm not sure I'd be able to let go.

Coming back down the stairs with a black box covered in cartoon bones in her hand, she said, "This looks fun," and took her seat again.

It was a game. I read the title out loud: "Skeletons In Your Closet."

"Have you ever played it before?"

I shook my head. "Never heard of it."

Reading the box, she recited, "Get to know the people you think you already know."

"Sounds dangerous," I said. "Is this the part in the horror movie where I find out you've committed murder before?"

She gasped. "Come on. It was only that one time."

"I'm sure he had it coming."

Shaking the box with a wicked glint in her eye, she asked, "Want to?"

Hell yes, I did. Whatever it was, I wanted to. "Sure," I said, then I leaned forward, lowered my voice, and waggled my brows. "Especially if *bones* are involved."

She blew air through her lips at my bad joke, and I got to my feet.

"Where are you going?" she asked, gazing up at me.

At this angle, I could have, but expressly did not stare down into her cleavage when I said, "I'll play your little game, Hannah. But if my skeletons are about to come out, I need another beer first."

CHAPTER EIGHT

HANNAH

He added wood to the fire while the wind whipped up outside. And I wondered if it would ever stop raining. I kind of hoped it wouldn't. I hoped raindrops against glass, wood crackling in the stove, and Joey snoring in his chair would be the soundtrack of our entire weekend.

"More wine?" he asked from the kitchen.

"Yes, please," I answered, and he came around the counter to fill my glass.

Setting the wine bottle down on the table, he sat across from me with his full beer and asked, "How do we play?"

"Well, there's dice and a board and these little bone pieces."

His brow floated up, and I rolled my eyes. Even though he was hardly the only person at this table with bone on the brain.

"I think we should just ask the questions on the cards," I suggested. "I don't care about keeping score, and that way we don't have to move the puzzle."

"Fair enough," he said. "Who goes first?"

"Oldest?"

Sitting back in his chair, he spread his legs wide, crossed his arms over his chest, and said, "I'm ready. Hit me."

Slowly, for dramatic effect, I pulled out a card, read the question, and burst into laughter.

"What?" When he leaned forward, I leaned back.

"No. No peeking." I smushed the card against my chest. "Just... give me a second."

He rested his elbow on the table, patiently cradling his cheek in his palm. And why was that so sexy? Why was everything he did so sexy?

"Okay." Taking a deep, steadying breath, I read aloud, "When shit gets real, what's your"—I paused, struggling not to crack up again —"most unhinged coping strategy?"

He stared at me. I stared at him. And then we both devolved into giggles.

"This is a joke," he said. "You're making this up."

Passing him the card, I wiped the tears from my eyes.

He handed me the card back, cleared his throat, and said, "Well. Since we both already know *your* answer, little missy."

"Stop," I whimpered through my hands covering my face.

"Mine would be, um, well... It's actually kind of embarrassing."

Lowering my hands, I found him scratching his head. And was he flushed? I couldn't tell, so I grabbed the battery powered lantern on the table and raised it between us.

"What are you doing?"

"I'm trying to see if you're blushing. It's hard to tell in this light."

Taking my hand, he pressed my palm over his cheek, which was very warm, and admitted, "Like a schoolboy."

I wanted to brush my thumb over his skin. I wanted to curl my fingers around his neck and pull him close.

Instead, I lowered the lantern. He let go of my hand, and then he said, "Nobody in my life knows this about me. Nobody. So be kind, okay?"

"You don't have to tell me if you don't want to."

He scoffed at my offer. "This is only the first question. Please. Of course I'm answering it." Rolling his shoulders then cracking his neck, he said, "Okay, here we go. When shit gets real." He closed his eyes, and maybe it was the shadows from the lantern, but his lashes seemed impossibly long. "I drive out of town to somewhere nobody knows me, find a karaoke bar, and sing."

"You do?" I was shocked. No, shock wasn't a strong enough word for whatever I was. "You sing karaoke? To strangers?"

"What?" He shrugged, and I'd bet if I touched his cheek now, it would be on fire. "I like to lose myself in song. Is that so bad?"

"Bad?" I asked, incredulous. "No, it's not bad. It's literally the best thing I have ever heard in my entire life. And as far as coping strategies go, it's creative, healthy, cathartic. Just top tier all around. Also, I've heard you singing in here, and you have an amazing voice."

His lips curved in a way that had me thinking about lollipops and ice cream cones and other lickable things.

"So." I grabbed my wineglass, getting ready to guzzle. "What are your songs?"

"My songs?"

I sipped, swallowed, and then explained, "Your karaoke hits? What do you sing?"

"You really want to know?"

Lowering my glass, I said, "I think I might actually die if you don't tell me."

"That sounds serious."

I nodded gravely. "It is. And if somehow I survive, it will only be so I can wander around aimlessly forever wondering what Darryn Madigan sings at his super-secret Karaoke nights."

He narrowed his eyes at me and ran his thumb along his lower lip. I really thought he might not tell me until he said, "Mostly old country. Johnny Cash and Hank Williams. But sometimes, after a few beers, I might break out—No." He shook his head. "Nope, I can't tell you this. No way."

Practically lunging across the table, I took his hands in mine and pleaded, "Please. Please, please, please. Pretty, pretty please with—"

"Okay, fine." He blew out a breath. "When I'm really cooking, I sing Madonna."

"Madonna?" I gaped at him. "Like *the* Madonna? Madonna Louise Ciccone? The Queen of Pop? That Madonna?"

"Yep," he said, popping the P. "That Madonna."

Looking down at the puzzle-covered table, then back up at him, I said, "This is so surprising."

He laughed.

"Which song? Or is it songs? Do you have a Madonna repertoire?"

"There are three that I rotate."

My cheeks were sore from smiling, so I rubbed them while he said, "'Open Your Heart,' 'Like a Prayer,' and rarely, super rarely, I really can't express enough how rarely this happens, like maybe twice in my life—"

"Darryn, please." The suspense was killing me.

His jaw clenched, muscles tensing. Then he admitted, "'Ray of Light'."

My eyes flared. I opened my mouth, closed it again. I imagined him up on a stage in some small-town bar with the bass thumping and the crowd going wild and his head tilting back and—

"You okay over there?"

"It's just...that song. I mean, it's a total banger, but it's so hard. All those high notes."

"Tell me about it."

"Do you try to hit them?"

"Try?" He leaned forward, locked eyes with me, and said, "Hannah, I nail them."

Every inch of my skin pulled tight at his low, rumbling voice. And with as much sincerity as I'd ever felt about anything, I said, "I am so happy right now."

He rolled his eyes, then he snatched the box of question cards from my side of the table. "All right, you. That's enough Darryn roasting for one night." His smirk was vengeful. "My turn."

I took another big sip of wine, preparing myself as he silently read a card, frowned at it, and put it back.

"Hey," I said. "That's cheating."

"No it isn't." He picked up another card, read the question, and put that one back too. "It's curating. Ah." His eyes sparkled. "Because this?" He tapped the next card to his lips. "This is the one."

My nerves skyrocketed for multiple reasons as I said a shaky "okay.

"It's a three-parter."

"Of course it is."

He looked at the card, then up at me, then back to the card and read, "In three words or less, what do other people think you're like? What do you think you're like? And what are you really like?"

"Uh..." I hedged, stalling. "Can you repeat the middle part?"

Grinning around his beer bottle, he took a sip.

"This is such a stress question," I grumbled, then sat up tall like I was about to defend a thesis. This shouldn't have felt so hard, but it did. Painfully hard. "Okay," I began, "other people might say that I'm competent, trustworthy, and maybe a little guarded. What?" I said when his brow floated up like *Guarded? You don't say?* "Don't give me that look."

"Sorry." With a remorseful wince, he nodded at me. "Go on. What do you think you're like?"

"I think," I chewed on my cheek, wading through my greatest and worst personality hits until I settled on "that I'm thoughtful, careful, and probably a perfectionist."

"I see," he said, keeping his expression comically neutral. "And who are you really, Hannah James?"

Who was I really? I looked up at the ceiling, like the answer might be carved into one of the beams. "I honestly have no idea."

Leaning forward, he rested his elbows on the table, dislodging several puzzle pieces from their spots, and asked, "Do you want to know who I think you are?"

Did I? What if it was bad? What if it would be like my last

performance review, when the principal praised me for being direct and assertive only to soften the blow of suggesting I take it down a notch at meetings? Was I about to spend weeks in crisis mode wondering if every facial expression I made or word I said was too bitchy? Was Darryn a backhanded compliment type of guy?

No. No, I didn't think so.

Girding my loins, I hauled my armor into place and said, "Okay."

He rolled his lips together, tilted his head, and set his undivided attention on me. "I think you are compassionate, loyal, and incredibly generous with everyone around you."

Well, that's not so bad—

"But I think you might not be very generous with yourself."

After taking a beat to pat myself down emotionally, I realized I wasn't hurt, only stunned. Because while it wasn't a backhanded compliment, it might have been something even worse: true.

"You okay?" he asked as I dropped my head and muttered, "Cellophane."

"What's that?" When I didn't answer him, because my heart was doing really weird things inside my chest and I thought it might be important to pay attention to them, he asked, "Did I go too far? I'm sorry. I just noticed—"

"No, it's fine." I reached for his hand again, needing to touch him for some reason. "You're just... You're not wrong."

He ran his thumb over my knuckles, and it felt so good that I immediately wanted to pull away. Which was the point. The whole entire fucking point. I wasn't generous with myself. I didn't let myself do things that felt good. Not usually. I didn't give myself permission to let my guard down and sink into bliss or joy or even simple contentment. As much as I encouraged others to embrace the good in their lives, I was always a little distrustful of anything that might be good in mine.

I had no idea when this change had happened in me or why. Maybe the divorce. Maybe motherhood. Maybe just age and experience hardening my shell. But I wanted to be okay with feeling good again. I wanted to trust. I wanted to trust him, specifically, this man I barely knew. I wanted to trust that even if I let myself sink into him, he'd make sure that this moment, this weekend, the memory I'd have of him when it was all over, would stay good.

So I kept my hand in his, letting myself indulge in this one good thing. And I told him, "It feels like you see me in a way other people don't. And sometimes it makes me uncomfortable. That's all."

"Hannah." His voice was low and soft and genuine. "I don't want to make you uncomfortable. Not unless you want me to." His brow flicked up. "The tickle fight is still on the table."

Laughing him off while my insides fizzed, I pulled my hand out of his and picked another card.

"Oh, this one's easy," I said while he cracked his knuckles. "What was your best Halloween costume?"

He scoffed. "How is that in any way a skeleton someone might be hiding in their closet?"

"You can't have a game that's all embarrassing secrets," I said with a shrug. "You gotta have some layups."

"Good point." He pursed his lips. "Let's see. I've had a lot of great costumes. I love Halloween. But probably, yeah, the year I went as a nudist colony."

My eyes popped. "A nudist colony?"

"I wore it to work too. So unprofessional."

"How?" I asked as a picture of him standing at the water cooler without a stitch of clothing on developed in my mind.

Sitting back, he narrowed his eyes at me. "You're imagining me naked now, aren't you?"

"I mean, pretty much," I admitted.

"I have done some wild shit in my day," he said with a chuckle, "but going to work naked is, sadly, not on that list. I got these beach-themed swim trunks and a tan tank top, then I taped naked Barbie and Ken dolls all over my body. My coworkers and clients thought it was hysterical, but Jeremiah, who was thirteen or so at the time, was mortified."

"Tell me you have pictures saved on your phone," I begged, practically lunging across the table. "Please."

Swiping his phone off the counter, he scrolled and scrolled and scrolled. And then he stopped, raised his head, and said, "Yep."

"Gimme!"

He was a bit younger in the picture, a bit leaner, still gorgeous. And the costume that included not only dolls, but beach chairs and beach balls too, was truly phenomenal. "This is amazing."

"What was your best costume?" he asked while I handed him his phone.

"It's nowhere near as good as yours, but when William was two, I got big into crocheting, and I made myself a flower hat and made him a honeybee suit. I was really proud of those costumes."

"Do you have pictures?"

"Even better," I said, and he got a little misty eyed when I found the video of William toddling around the yard, pretending to fly with his little crocheted wings.

"God, they're so cute at that age." He sniffled. "Jeremiah is still single, but I gotta tell you, I can't fucking wait to be a grandpa."

I could see it too, Grandpa Darryn giving piggyback rides and making bear-shaped pancakes, doing pushups while his grandkids sat on his back and giggled. It was all very sweet, very adorable, and very counterproductive to stemming my desire to ask him to take all his clothes off for real.

"Not me," I said, pretending I didn't think about it from time to time. "Both William and I are *way* too young."

With a twinkle in his eye, he said, "I don't know. He's only four years younger than I was when we had J."

My gasp was audible. "Why would you say that to me? That is pure nightmare fuel."

Snorting, he shrugged, then picked another card.

After several rounds of pulling and replacing cards until we found the best questions for each other, he learned that I once had a date with a guy that was so bad I accused him of being hired by my friends to punk me, and I learned that he once had a mullet. He learned that I'm weirdly terrified of getting caught in escalator teeth, and I learned that his first crush had been on his third-grade teacher, Miss Johnson.

We also found out that we shared the same comfort actor: John Candy. Darryn loved *Planes, Trains and Automobiles* the most. It was *Uncle Buck* for me. And we'd both cried when he died. We found out that we both voted democrat and made regular donations to our local food banks and NPR stations. And that while neither of us were religious, we both found something sacred in swimming in oceans and hiking up mountains and staring at the stars.

Eventually, we put the best get-to-know-you game in the world away and turned our attention back to the puzzle. But it didn't take long before my eyelids grew heavy, and the pieces blurred together in my tired vision. And then he yawned.

"Should we go to bed?" I asked, and Joey, hearing me, hopped down from his chair and trotted toward Darryn's door.

He took a moment to respond, and in that moment, I could see him struggling with how he wanted to handle my mistake. Because I hadn't said that *I* should go to bed. I'd said *we*, and it was an unintended invitation. In the end, he didn't take it. He only yawned again and said, "Yeah. I'm sleepy."

And thank goodness he did. Because going to bed with him tonight was pretty much all I'd thought about since he admitted to belting out Madonna to strangers when he was sad. I just wanted to sleep with him, curl up next to him, keep the warm and contented feeling after sitting across from this walking Xanax of a man all night going until sunrise. But I needed to be strong. We'd made it this far.

My knees creaked when I stood from the table. And after one last trip to the outhouse, I picked Joey up to give him a hug and said, "Good night, Darryn," while passing him his dog.

He replied, "Have sweet dreams, Hannah." Then I went to my room and he went to his, and I spent the next five minutes smiling into my pillow before falling into the second deepest sleep I'd had in years.

Until something woke me up.

"No" came a pained, broken plea in the darkness. "Don't."

I reached for my phone on my nightstand and disconnected it from the power bank. When I unlocked the screen, 3:23 a.m. glowed back at me. It was otherwise pitch-black in my room, so I turned on the phone's flashlight and called out, "Darryn? Are you okay?"

A soft whine answered.

I opened my door to find Joey sitting outside, waiting for me with wide, troubled eyes. He barked once, then turned around and led me down the stairs to Darryn's room.

His door was open, and when I shined the flashlight inside, I could see him, asleep on his belly, his back muscles tensed, one knee bent up, the covers thrown off.

"No," he groaned while his foot twitched. "Stop."

Walking around the bed to turn on his lamp, I sank to my knees beside him. His brows were pulled tight, his eyes flicking from side to side beneath his closed lids. Just like William's used to do when he had night terrors.

"Darryn." I touched his shoulder. "Wake up. You're having a nightmare." When that didn't work, I gave him a little shake.

His eyes opened with a flash, and when he saw me, recognized me, they closed again as he sucked in a lungful of air. "Fuck." He pressed his forehead into his pillow. "Did I wake you?"

"Are you okay?"

"Yeah, um. Just a bad dream." Rolling onto his side, he rubbed his eyes. "I still get them sometimes, about being...over there. I'm sorry I woke you."

"Don't be sorry," I said, because why was he apologizing to me? "Can I do anything for you? Get you some water or—"

"No. I'm okay." I'm sure he hoped his thin smile would reassure me, but it didn't. I had a stoic kid. I knew the deal. "I'll be fine."

I brushed his curls off his forehead. But before I could pull away, he trapped my hand with his and brought my knuckles to his lips.

"Maybe there is something you can do for me," he said, kissing my knuckles one at a time.

"Darryn." I clung to caution by my fingernails, maybe just one fingernail, the pinky. "We shouldn't—"

Meeting my stare, he said, "No, not that. But could you sleep with me? Just sleep?" He pressed my hand over his still-pounding heart. "It helps."

Faced with his sleepy eyes and beating heart and vulnerable everything else, how could I say no?

Cupping his cheek, I said, "Okay." Then I turned off the lamp, pulled the covers back over him, and walked to my side of the bed. When I notched in behind him, he reached back for me, pulled my arm over his side, and tucked our clasped hands under his chin. His body was big and warm, and his hair smelled like woodsmoke and rain. When I cuddled even closer, touching him in as many places at once as I could, he hummed, like it felt as good to him as it did to me.

A person might see us and think I was being generous with someone else again. But being in his bed with my arm wrapped around him, feeling his chest rise and fall with each breath he took, I was being generous with myself too, and I think we both knew it.

Nestled against him with our fingers intertwined and Joey curled up at our feet, I fell asleep quickly. Later, Darryn would tell me that he didn't dream again that night.

But I did.

I dreamed of hands on my body, moving me, putting me where they wanted me. I dreamed of blue eyes gazing down at me. Of hips nestled firmly between mine, lips on my skin, a tongue licking, teeth grazing, something hard and thick pressing into me. I dreamed of pushing back against it, rocking my hips into it. I sighed, and he hummed. And that's when I realized I wasn't dreaming at all.

"Morning," Darryn murmured behind me.

We must have switched places during the night, because I was the small spoon now, and he was everywhere. Legs, arms, chest, cock. Warm, strong, hard. Everywhere.

His hand was on my stomach, holding me, urging me closer to the rigid length at my back. My body responded to his touch like it was a promise whispered in my ear: This will feel so good.

God, I wanted him. I wanted him so badly I couldn't breathe. I wasn't sure if he was fully awake yet or still half asleep, which made me want him even more. He was so warm. So soft and hard all at once. And I loved warm, soft, lazy morning sex the way some people loved chocolate brownie sundaes. Enough to throw years of making good decisions down the drain for one single delicious bite.

I was starved for this feeling, this wanting, and he was offering me ice cream and chocolate and a bright red cherry on top. Maybe I should stop thinking so much. Maybe I should just...bite.

Reaching back, I slid my hand over his thigh and pulled him into me.

"Hannah." His lips dropped to my shoulder, his hand sliding lower on my stomach. "What are we doing?"

"I don't know," I breathed when he rocked into me and kissed my neck. "But it feels good."

"Fuck yes, it does," he hissed when my fingernails dug into his skin. "Are you sure, though? Yesterday, you didn't—"

"I'm sure." I melted into the bed when his fingers danced along the skin below my belly button. Between getting to know him better last night and how good his body felt molded to mine now, the only thing I didn't want was for him to stop. "I was wrong yesterday. I was overthinking everything. I want this. I need it."

When he hummed, "That's my good girl," I remembered.

He'd said those same words to me two days ago. They'd snapped something inside me then, like a rubber band pulled too tight. Now they pulled me tight again, making my clit throb and my nipples grow painfully hard.

"Can I touch you?" Taking the strap of my camisole between his teeth, he pulled it down over my shoulder, and I said, "Yes."

He slid his hand up under the hem of my top, and I closed my eyes when his fingers skated over my ribs, bit my lip when he palmed my breast, nearly combusted when his thumb rolled over my nipple. He was still in his sweats; I was fully dressed. The room was dim and silent, and somehow it all felt so naughty. Like we were getting away with something, hiding from the world with his arm around me and his chest behind me and his hips rolling into me as he kissed my shoulder, my neck, the spot behind my ear.

"Tell me to stop," he warned as he moved his hand down my stomach again, his fingers dipping under my waistband.

"I won't," I promised. Then I gave him full permission by pushing his hand into my pants.

Whispering my name, he cupped me, his long fingers dragging through my center. And he was so good at this, at knowing exactly what I needed without me having to tell him. Knowing that, *yes*, I wanted one finger inside me, and then two. Just like that. And, *god yes*, sliding up to my clit now, moving over me, a light pressure, a slow, mind-numbing pace. And, *yes*, his hips holding a steady rhythm, his hard cock rocking against me, reminding me how good it felt when he was inside me. Making me want it again.

His fingers circled faster, and I reached up to grasp his neck, holding on while he drove me so close to the edge there was nowhere to go but over. And when he pressed down on me, suspending me in midair until my clit pulsed like an unbearable heartbeat, I nearly begged him for release. But then, like he knew, like he sensed my body starting to panic, he lightened his pressure and circled his fingers again, fast and steady until my eyes closed, my belly pulled tight, and I cried out as a bright and delicious release tore through me.

Listening to me, making me come, thrusting against me, it must have worked for him too. Because he wasn't done. He wasn't ramping down. He was wild.

And it was phenomenal.

Cupping me again, holding me still as he moved his hips harder, faster, his rhythm became erratic, his breath rasping in my ear. When

I pushed back on him, meeting him thrust for thrust, his teeth sank into my shoulder as a deep, satisfied, and incredibly sexy grunt rumbled through his chest.

Neither of us had removed a single article of clothing, and that was still the hottest thing that had happened to me in...ever.

Eventually, after we caught our breaths and I came back down to this planet, he pulled me close and growled into my ear, "You just made me come in my pants."

A laugh trickled out of me. And when I said, "I really love this for us," he laughed too.

"Are you still okay?" he asked, hesitant now that our brains were functioning again.

Was I? Was I still okay? Was this the terrible idea I'd convinced myself it was going to be? Maybe, at least a little, because if I could see inside my chest right now, my heart would probably be glowing. I doubted there was a feeling left anywhere in the room because I'd caught them all. But if I just kept my head clear, kept reminding myself that this was only for the weekend, kept telling myself that he was, in every way I could imagine, worth it, I could get out of this cabin in one piece. I could go home knowing that I'd embraced the kind of experience people wrote books about. As long as I could keep everything contained to the next twenty-four hours, I was still okay.

So I rolled over, and when he looped his arm around my waist, yanking me close, I said, "I am." I slid my hand over his cheek, loving the rasp of his stubble against my palm. "But you were right last night. I'm not very good at being generous with myself. And being here, being with you like this, it feels generous. It feels big and indulgent and a little too good to be true. So it scared me. I'm sorry if I seem confusing."

"No." His eyes went soft. "You're not confusing. But I don't want you to be scared, Hannah. I don't want you to regret anything about this weekend. About"—his throat worked through a swallow—"me."

"I don't think I will," I said. And to prove it to him, I leaned in and kissed him. I kissed him the same way he'd kissed me, first on one corner of his mouth, and then the other. I brushed my tongue over the seam of his lips, and he rolled on top of me, settling between my legs as he deepened the kiss, turning my entire body molten. And I thought, *I could stay here all day*. All day just kissing him, touching him, letting him kiss and touch me back.

"Hannah?" he said against my lips, kissing me again, over and over until I was dizzy.

"Yes?" I said when he finally let me come up for air.

Gazing down at me, resting his weight on his elbows, already hard again and letting me know it with a slow press of his hips, he asked, "Does this mean we can turn PeePaw's into a fuck cabin now?"

The smile that overcame me, it was like joy, like light pouring out of me, like levitating. And when I said, "Yes," he kissed me fiercely. But I was messy. *We* were messy.

"Darryn?" I asked while he pushed my cami up over my breasts, kissing and nuzzling and sucking. "Is there a way to shower here?"

With a slow, hot swipe of his tongue over my nipple, he gazed up at me through his long lashes and said, "No running water, remember?"

"I know. But when I first saw you, you had a towel around your waist, and you were"—I moaned when he swirled his tongue around my other nipple—"all wet."

"Ah, right. The creek."

"The creek? The one outside?" I frowned, because the creek outside was not only shallow, but really fucking cold too. "Seriously?"

Raising his head, he said, "I know, it's cold. But the rain has stopped, the sun is finally shining, and the birds are singing." He moved up my body, peppering my lips with soft, lingering kisses. "And I promise I'll warm you up after."

CHAPTER NINE

DARRYN

WITH HER HAND IN MINE, I led Hannah along the creek beside the cabin. The water was crystal clear, the early morning sunlight reflecting off the ripples like glitter, and I felt like that sunlight. I felt like I'd won the fucking lottery, summitted Everest, nailed that final high note in "Ray of Light" in front of a crowd of thousands. And it wasn't just that she'd let me touch her and make her come again. That was great, don't get me wrong. But she'd kissed me. *She'd* kissed me, which was an important distinction.

I knew she wasn't the only one here taking a risk, the only one who should be scared. There was something between us, something real and undeniable. Something more than enjoying all the potential perks of unfettered access to a fuck cabin. But I didn't care. I didn't fucking care. I just wanted her. I wanted her for as long as she'd let me have her. Sneaking up on fifty made a person realize real quick that they wouldn't live forever. So I'd live the next twenty-four hours with her—preferably without any clothes on—like they were all I had left, and I'd deal with the fallout later.

"It's just over here." I ducked into the trees, guiding her to the deep pool I'd found several years ago in the back corner of PeePaw's property. In the clearing, mountains rose to the east while the sun started its slow climb over their jagged, rocky peaks. And all around us, aspens quaked in the breeze, their tallest branches glowing yellow and orange.

"This is so beautiful," she said.

I swept a glance her way. "It's even more beautiful now."

She turned toward me, her cheeks turning pink either from the morning chill or from my compliment, and asked, "How cold is it?"

"Only one way to find out." Standing beside the water, I pushed my pants down and kicked them off. Then I stood in front of her. Completely naked. In broad daylight. Which was a lot more daunting than I thought it would be.

Her wide eyes raked me over from head to toe as she bit her lip. Slowly, she shook her head, setting all my insecurities to rest when she said, "Darryn, you are *so* fucking hot."

Pointing my chin her way, I said, "Your turn. Or do you want me to turn around?"

She took a deep breath, let it out slowly, and yanked her top off over her head. I forgot to breathe while she slid her pants down over her hips and stepped out of them.

"Do you have any idea how gorgeous you are?" I asked her while she stood still for me.

She smiled, and there we were, both naked, our bodies bathed in sunlight, and even though it might have been a bad idea, even if it was way too much honesty this early in the morning, I said, "I really don't understand how you showed up here. I don't know if it was fate or just luck. But I wasn't excited to come up this weekend. I didn't want the silence like I usually do. I didn't want to be alone. I wanted...you, I guess." I squeezed the back of my neck. "That probably sounds crazy."

"It doesn't," she said quickly, stepping toward me. And it felt like she wanted to say more, admit some things too, but she didn't let herself.

Reaching out, brushing the backs of my fingers over her cheek, I said, "It's okay. I just needed to get that out."

The way she looked at me then, like she still wasn't sure if I was a real person, made me chuckle. "Come on, Hannah," I said, turning toward the water, ready to dive in. "Let's get wet."

"Fuck!" she cried out when she finally jumped in after me. "It's freezing!"

"Oh, it's not so bad." I dunked beneath the surface, then popped back up with a sharp, pained gasp. "Okay, it's pretty bad," I admitted, wiping my eyes dry. And then my attention snagged helplessly on the droplets of water traveling between her breasts, beading on the tips of her tight, hard nipples. "But it's better after you've gone down—I mean under. It's better after you've gone under."

She held her breath, slammed her eyes shut, and sank. When she came back up again, I was there, right in front of her, pulling her into my arms.

"That wasn't so bad, was it?"

Wrapping her legs around my waist, she said, "It was the worst." And then she kissed me. When her lips parted, I swept my tongue inside, losing myself in the warm softness of her mouth. The current was light, barely moving in our little pool, and I held her hips steady as she let go of me and laid back, as the water swept her arms out to the sides, her hair flowing all around her in dark brown waves.

I dragged my hand down between her breasts, growing hard against her as birds sang above us. The water suspended her body at the perfect height, and it would be so easy to slide inside her this way. She was right there, so soft and perfect. All I'd have to do was line myself up, hold her hips in place, and push.

"I really want to fuck you like this." My voice rasped out like gravel. "The way you look right now, with your hair streaming behind you and your nipples so tight and your skin so pebbled. It's pornographic, Hannah."

"You can," she said to the sky, so quietly I wondered if I'd imagined it.

"I can? I can fuck you?"

"Yes."

I clenched my jaw so tightly something popped, then gritted out, "I don't have a condom."

"We don't need one," she said while my cock went rock hard. "I can't get pregnant anymore. And I don't have any STIs. Unless you do."

"I don't." I reached one hand up between her shoulder blades, supporting her as I leaned over her body. "But are you sure?"

"I'm sure. Ah," she gasped when I sucked her cold nipple into my mouth. "Yes, please."

"Thank you, Hannah. Thank you." It was all I could say, because it was all I could think while I dragged the head of my erection through her center. That and "You're so slippery. I could just slide right in."

She responded by cinching her legs around my waist, pulling me closer. I didn't know if it was possible for her to want this as much as I did, maybe not even half as much. But the possibility that she might, the water rippling and the sun shining and her perfect mouth opening on a gasp as I pushed into her, was enough to nearly set me off.

I slid out to the tip, then thrust into her again, deeper this time. And it all felt so good. The cold water. Her warm body. Her soft muscles gripping me with nothing between us but skin.

"Fuck, Hannah." I grasped her hips, sliding so deeply inside her I bottomed out. "Can you feel that? Can you feel how hard you make me?"

Closing her eyes, tilting her head back so her chin caught the light, she said, "You feel so good. It's perfect."

It was perfect. So hot and perfect with her eyes closed, her lips wet, her tits bouncing with each snap of my hips, the little moans rising from her throat. I wasn't going to last.

What was wrong with me? Where was my legendary stamina? If my partner wanted me to, I could usually go for hours. But not with her. Not with Hannah. At least not yet. Maybe that was it. Maybe I just needed more of her. Maybe I needed to make love to her all day, not letting her lift a finger until she'd had at least six orgasms. No, seven. Fuck, oh god. My balls pulled tight, sensation gathering like a storm in the base of my spine.

"I'm sorry," I said, driving into her harder, faster, digging my fingers into her hips. "I'm close. Should I pull out when—"

"No." She opened her eyes and found mine. "Stay. I want to feel you when you come."

I want to feel you when you come? Was she kidding me? Saying something like that while I was holding on for dear life? I'd be lucky if I lasted another five seconds.

"Are you warm enough?" I asked, or at least I think I did. My brain-mouth coordination was questionable at best.

She nodded, and when I thrust into her again, her back bowed, that little divot sinking between her brows.

"Can you come again?" I asked.

"I...ah, I don't know."

That wasn't good enough. So I slowed my pace, just a little, pulling back, then going deep, then shallow again. "Hannah?"

Her legs trembled around me, and when I stayed shallow, angling my hips to apply pressure along her front wall, she cried out, "Yes."

That's more like it.

"Touch yourself," I said, picking up my pace, holding her still, sliding in and out a little deeper each time. "Come with me."

And I knew that this, right here, right now, watching her reach between our bodies, watching her tease herself while she stared up at me and I stared down at her like nobody else existed in the entire universe except for us, like no other time existed in history except for this moment, would ruin me.

Of course it would be her, this woman I couldn't have. There was a reason they called these sorts of experiences once in a lifetime. Nobody got to keep them.

With my next thrust, her walls closed in around me and her legs gripped my waist. She cried out my name, and I was gone. My hips snapped, eyes closed, heart nearly exploding as I came for what felt like minutes, emptying myself into her until I could barely see. Until I could barely stand. But I fought through it all, holding her, supporting her, keeping her afloat. And when I found my bearings again, my vision cleared, my heartbeat slowed, everything slowed. Everything but the water, the clouds, our breaths.

I gathered her into my arms. Her skin was cold, so I pressed her tightly against my chest while thoughts swam through my head. Words I couldn't say. *I've never felt this way about anyone before. Why do you fit so perfectly in my arms? I think you're who I've spent my entire life searching for.*

No, I couldn't say those things. It was ridiculous to even think them. So I cupped her head as her arms closed around me, as she nestled her nose into the crook of my neck. And when she pulled back, kissed me softly, then looked at me with something in those deep brown eyes that felt genuine, felt real, I knew one thing for certain.

I was so fucked.

CHAPTER TEN

HANNAH

I was so fucked.

"What's your safe word?" he asked, his eyes pitch-black and penetrating as he appraised me without an ounce of mercy.

"Stop!" Tears streamed down my face, my body convulsing, chest heaving.

"No, sweetheart. That's not it."

"It's—ah!" I erupted into another spasm of laughter while he went to work on my sides, my ribs, while his thighs squeezed my legs together so tightly I couldn't move. "Kumquat!"

"That's right." His fingers assaulted my armpits, and I screamed. "Need to use it?"

I shook my head vigorously, refusing to give him the satisfaction. Until he reached back and started in on my feet.

"Darryn!"

"Yes?"

I couldn't answer, couldn't see, could barely breathe.

"Oh, Hannah. You sweet summer child. I've had a lifetime of honing my tickle fighting skills. A novice like you?" He clicked his tongue. "You never stood a chance."

The hell I didn't.

He might have one up on me when it came to tickle fights, but he was a nice guy. I wasn't nice. I fought dirty. And at his first mistake, a momentary pause while he sat back and let me catch my breath, I went in for the kill.

Reaching down, I yanked up my shirt. And when his eyes dropped to my breasts, his pupils flaring, focus successfully snagged, I twisted as hard as I could to the side and jerked my legs out from under him. Whipping my body around until I was on all fours, I reveled in his shocked expression and lunged for him.

"No! Stop! Not my ribs!" he cried out, collapsing onto his back while I straddled him and pinned his arms down with my knees.

"Pretty sure I didn't hear a safe word in there," I teased before digging my fingertips into his sides and dropping my head to let the ends of my hair tickle his face.

"Ca-Cas—" he tried to say, laughing too hard to get the word out.

"What's that?" I tickled him a little harder. "I can't hear you."

"Cassiopeia!" His eyes glistened. "You evil woman."

Still straddling him as he pulled his arms free of my thighs and gripped my hips, I asked, "Did I win?"

"The tickle fight?"

I nodded, and his eyes shifted between mine, then his gaze slid down my nose, over my cheeks, my lips, slow and careful like he was memorizing every detail, committing each of my freckles to memory, documenting the length of my eyelashes. "Yeah, Hannah," he said. "You won."

"You have the most amazing eyes," I told him, trying to commit him to memory too. "They're so blue. It's like looking at the sky."

"You can thank my father for those. He passed them down to all four of us boys."

"What a gift." When his erection stirred against my ass, I said, "You also have an amazing dick."

His nose crinkled, his cheeks flushing above his stubble. "I hate to say it, but..."

"Wow," I said, elated. "Thank you again, Daddy Madigan." And the thought, *I'd like to meet him someday*, was suddenly so loud in my head that whatever self-preserving instincts I had left rushed to change the subject. Which wasn't too difficult.

Because Darryn was hard. And I was ready. And he was so beautiful lying there on his back, staring up at me while his expression turned hungry.

I reached between our bodies, took him in hand, and sank slowly down onto him. Slow enough that my thighs burned. His eyes fluttered, and his fingers closed around my hips, pleading with me to let him in. But he didn't push me down or thrust up into me. He was patient, careful. Between this morning in the creek and twice already in his bed after we got back to the cabin, I hadn't had this much sex in years, and it burned a little as he stretched me.

"Are you sore?" he asked as I finally settled into his lap.

"A little." Hinging forward, I pressed my body against his while he wrapped his arms around me.

Rolling his hips slowly beneath me, he said, "Me too. But it feels good."

It did feel good. So good that I wanted to be sore like this all the time. I wanted to feel the imprint of him inside me every waking moment of every day. I was on the verge of doing something ill-advised like telling him that when he rolled me over and pulled out.

"What are you doing?" I whined. "I want you to fuck me."

"Soon." He kissed me deeply, then he slid down my body. When he kissed my breasts, my belly, the point of my hip, the crease of my thigh, I shut my mouth.

Spreading my legs apart, flattening onto his belly between them, he said, "You didn't let me do this before." He stared between my thighs the way he had our first time together, focused and ravenous. "Can I do it now?"

"Yes," I said while he parted me with his thumbs. "Please."

He hummed, and when he hoisted my hips into the air and licked me, his flat, warm tongue sliding from my perineum all the way to my clit, I fell back onto the bed. It shouldn't have surprised me that he'd be good at this. He was good at everything. And I don't know if it was because he knew I was sore, but no man had ever been so soft with me, so slow and patient and sweet. I was being adored, savored, and despite his careful pace, or maybe because of it, I was close before I wanted to be.

A tight, tingling sensation swirled deep in my belly. And after another slow lick, the tip of his tongue flicking over my clit, his finger teasing my entrance, I was already balancing on the edge.

"Wait." I pushed his head away. "Stop."

Gazing up at me between my thighs, his eyes glazed over, he asked, "Are you okay?"

"Yeah." I willed my heart to slow. "I'm okay. You're just kind of amazing at this and…" I didn't want to say that I was trying to slow time, to make every moment with him last as long as possible before the sun came up and we left this place. That seemed too real, too sad. So I only said, "I'm not ready to come yet."

"Ah." His lips curled, eyes clearing. "I love this game." He slid a finger inside me, dragging the tip along my front wall. "I can play this game for hours."

After a moment of slowly stroking me, pumping a finger in and out of me while the electric crackling throughout my body faded to a low buzz, he raised his brows in question, and I nodded.

It didn't take long before I writhed and bucked and pushed him off me again. He waited patiently, sucking and nibbling on my inner thighs while I caught my breath, while the bright, intense throbbing between my legs dimmed to a deep, dull ache.

"Okay," I said, and he went back to work.

With one finger still inside me, he reached up with his other hand and palmed my breast. When he closed his lips around my clit and sucked, rolling my nipple at the same time, I wasn't sure I'd have the luxury of backing away from the edge again. But I wanted to. I wanted more, longer, forever. And right before I pushed him back again, he pulled away on his own, pulled out of me, like he knew how close I was. Like he'd learned.

My hips rose helplessly into the air, searching for friction, a finger, a tongue, a breath, anything.

"Shh, sweetheart," he soothed, his palm warm and heavy on my belly, pushing down, holding me still. "I'm hard as hell and leaking all over the place down here. Please tell me you're ready to come."

Through the edged-out haze, I panted up at the ceiling and said, "Okay. I'm ready." Then I gasped while he sucked hard enough on my thigh that I knew I'd have a bruise. And when he flicked his tongue over my clit again, I cried out.

Ten very loud seconds later, a climax so intense I was almost scared of it tore through me. It was a detonation, a celestial event. I even cried a little. Because how had he just given me the best orgasm of my life, and I was still supposed to say goodbye to him tomorrow?

Rising to his feet at the end of the bed, he flipped me over, pushed my knees up under me, and hauled my hips toward him. When he entered me from behind, spearing me in one sublime thrust, my brain emptied out, all thoughts and worries swirling away like water down a drain.

This sex wasn't sweet. It wasn't gentle. It was all-encompassing. It was his hand pushing down between my shoulder blades, his fingers digging into my hip. It was filthy grunts of praise and skin slapping against skin as he drove into me so fast and hard I could barely breathe. And it had been so long since I'd been fucked, *truly* fucked like this, that I almost cried again. Because it felt so good. So amazing. So real and raw and vital.

"Is this okay?" he asked, his voice juddering. "I can slow down—"

"Don't...you...dare," I got out with what little breath I could catch between thrusts.

"Fuck. Good. God. Hannah." His harsh words were kindling, lighting a fire inside me. But when he raised his hand from my back, smacked my ass once, then pushed me down to the bed again before somehow increasing his pace, I ignited, swept into another orgasm that felt as inevitable as thunder after a lightning strike.

Sweat slicked our bodies as my muscles melted beneath my skin. But he wasn't done yet. He pumped into me over and over, hard enough that I had to fist the sheets and hold on to keep him from fucking me up the bed. After two orgasms, it was almost too much. Almost too fast. Almost too hard. Almost. And just when I felt like I couldn't take any more, like I was losing myself, sinking so deeply into some thoughtless, formless abyss I wasn't sure I'd ever come back up, he jerked, bucked, and bit out a string of curses I barely heard over the blood roaring in my ears.

His hips slowed, and then they stilled. And then he collapsed on top of me, covering me, giving me form and shape again with his weight, his harsh breaths, his curls brushing against my cheek.

"Christ," he slurred. "I think I'm dead."

I missed his weight the second he rolled off me.

"Are you okay?" he asked as he smoothed his hand over my sweat-soaked skin, stroking up and down my back. "That got a little rough. Was it too much?"

"Are you kidding?" My face was half smushed into the mattress, my arms splayed wide, hair everywhere, an endorphin-fueled, blissed-out afterglow infusing every cell in my body. "You can fuck me like that anytime you want."

He didn't make a sound, didn't sigh or even hum like he sometimes did. So I turned my head, wondering if he'd passed out from exhaustion after working so hard. But when he swept my hair out of my eyes, and I could finally see him, my heart broke at his expression.

"Anytime," he repeated sadly, a corner of his mouth pulling tight.

I felt it too, the ache. Because we didn't have anytime. We had less than a day.

Rolling onto my side, I took his hand in mine. I wished I knew what to say, something simple and true that would make us both feel better. But nothing came to me. Nothing must have come to him either. And after a long, silent moment, he sighed and said, "You should probably pee. You haven't in a while, and with how much sex we've been having..."

"What a king." I let go of his hand to brush my fingers over his cheek. "Puts me through the mattress all day long *and* looks out for my lady parts."

Leaning in, he kissed me softly, and then, because it was something he did so well, he lightened the mood. "Helper-therapy principle strikes again." His lips tipped into a sleepy, sex-drunk smile. "Because the benefits of your pussy are definitely not one-sided."

After a few more stolen moments of laughing and smiling and tangled limbs and tongues, he threw on a pair of jeans while I wrapped myself up in one of his flannel shirts. When we came back inside from relieving ourselves—me in the outhouse, Darryn and Joey in the trees—we realized we'd spent so much of the day in bed that we'd forgotten to eat.

Connecting my phone to his Bluetooth, I fired up my "Summer Road Trip" playlist. Then I made grilled cheese sandwiches and tomato soup while he worked on the puzzle and Joni Mitchell asked if we wanted to take a chance.

Which was, ironically, what I'd been asking myself too while I watched him.

His hair was post-sex messy, his stubble so long now it bordered on scruff, and he hadn't bothered putting on a shirt. Which I appreciated, because his body was mesmerizing. *He* was mesmerizing. Every vein, every muscle, every little gesture that seemed so uniquely Darryn. Rubbing his eyebrow, squeezing his neck, tapping his fingers on the table. I couldn't look away. Even when he caught me staring, even when I nearly burned our sandwiches, I couldn't look away from him.

Memory was precarious, imperfect. If I didn't pay close attention, would I remember the tiny freckle on his cheek? Or the precise angle of his jaw? When my mind reconstructed his mouth, would his lower lip be as full? Would his upper lip be so perfectly curved? When I dreamed about his eyes, would they stay so vibrantly blue? Or would the color fade over time?

"What are you thinking about?" he asked.

When I answered, sadly, saying, "Things I don't want to think about yet," he stood from the table, joined me in the kitchen, and pulled me into his arms.

We didn't speak, not then. We only held each other while I pressed my hands into his back, trying to memorize him that way too. The feel of his skin, the shape of his torso, the firmness of his chest. The solid and steady heartbeat thumping against my ear, sounding so much like *stay, stay, stay*.

CHAPTER ELEVEN

DARRYN

"We're almost done." She looked down at the seven remaining puzzle pieces with an unreadable expression.

Clearing something thick from my throat, I said, "Yep."

The last few pieces of a puzzle always came together faster than the first. Especially when all you wanted them to do was take as long as possible.

She placed a piece, I placed the next one, and on we went, silently taking turns, crawling toward the inevitable. It was actually a sad picture we were putting together, hard to look at. Two wolves on opposite sides of the frame, both howling mournfully at a full moon.

"You should do the last one." She slid the final piece over to me, even though it was her turn.

Shaking my head, I slid the piece back. "I've finished every single puzzle on that shelf. This one's for you." *So that next year, when I come up here again, I'll see the box and remember that it was you who completed it.*

She pressed the last piece into place, filling the empty, gaping hole in the middle of the bigger wolf's chest. And I thought, *I'm pretty sure I know how that feels, because she does that for me too.*

"Wanna get out of here?" I asked, needing a break, a change of scenery, fewer hopelessly romantic thoughts. "Hit the saloon for a drink?"

Maybe she needed a break too, because she was already on her feet when she replied, "Absolutely."

We took her car, which we were able to extricate easily from the rapidly drying mud, and all I could think about on the short drive to town was how much I wanted to hold her hand. Just intertwine my fingers with hers and hold on. But even after everything we'd done to each other, holding hands during a short drive felt too intimate. That was the sort of thing that couples did. Not two people who'd just met and might never see each other again after tomorrow.

"Let's stop in the General first," she said, parking the car while my throat closed up and my eyes misted over. "In case William texted back."

"Good idea." When she turned to me, her brows slid together. "Hey. You okay?"

"Oh, for sure," I lied, blinking hard. "Just some dust. Allergies, maybe."

She didn't believe me, I could tell. But she gave me a sad, understanding nod anyway, and we climbed out of the car.

"Hey, you two," the clerk chirped when we walked through the door. "I was wondering if I'd see you again."

While Hannah walked up to the counter to chat, I hoofed it to the beer fridge in the back of the store. I didn't really need beer. But I did need cold. I needed to open the door and stick my head inside until the icy air cleared my senses.

There we go. Just breathe. It's just Balsam Ridge magic. It's just the aftereffects of amazing sex. You are not falling in love with a woman you've known for two days. This isn't fucking Disney.

"I can't believe it." Hannah was absolutely beaming when she found me, which did not help my existential romantic crisis one bit. "William texted back. I mean, it's just a heart and thumbs-up emoji. But I'll take it."

Not that I'd really expected one, but I didn't have a single text or missed call waiting for me. Not even from Mom. Usually, this wouldn't have bothered me. I was a single guy. My kid was grown. My VA office was closed for the holiday. My brothers and friends were all busy with their own lives. But now there was this ache in my chest I had to swallow past before I could say, "That's awesome."

Still smiling, she sidled up next to me. "And Jane over there, that's the clerk's name," she said under her breath, "is pretty sure we're fucking."

I snorted. "Well, we *are* fucking. So..."

"Jane also thinks we should come back up here for our wedding."

Since it was supposed to be a joke, we laughed at it. But then, at the same time, we fell silent, our expressions shifting into something much more complicated.

"I'm, um, going to try to call William," she said, taking a step away from me.

I nodded, and when she walked toward the tourist T-shirts display, I stuck my head in the beer fridge again.

* * *

The saloon was packed, which made sense. After two days of rain, the sky was crystal clear, the sun was bright and warm, and everyone was out, shaking off their cabin fever. Teenagers huddled in loud groups by the tetherball court. Younger kids chased each other around the playground, their parents looking a little haggard and extremely grateful for the break from having to entertain them.

Hannah and I were lucky to find a small empty table under a cottonwood tree next to an older couple, probably in their late seventies. They were watching the kids play, their hands clasped across their table. I wondered if they'd met up here too. If fifty years ago, the Balsam Ridge Magic had gotten a hold of them and never let go.

"How was William?" I asked. Their phone call hadn't lasted very long, but Hannah had seemed a little distant ever since.

"He's good," she said before taking a sip of her drink. "He and his friends had been surfing all day, which was something I didn't even know he could do."

"He probably picked it up in a couple of hours," I said. "Oh, to be young."

A crease formed between her brows. It felt like a cloud passing over the sun. "And then he told me that his friend was upset because he'd found out his parents were moving to Boston. He was furious that they were selling his childhood home. William said they'd spent the entire afternoon trying to talk him down."

"Oof, that's rough," I said. "The childhood home is sacred. My parents still live in ours, but most people don't get to keep theirs. Most people only have memories."

"I didn't get to keep mine," she said distantly. And then, with a sharp inhale followed by a slow exhale, the cloud lifted, and she seemed to snap out of whatever had been bothering her. "Anyway"— she raised her eyes to the mountains—"what a gorgeous day."

"It's perfect," I said, my eyes set on her.

I wished we had one more day together. If we did, I'd offer to take her hiking. Or to rent stand-up paddleboards and head into the North Fork of Glacier National Park to one of the lakes. We could even drive over Going-to-the-Sun Road, look for wildflowers and mountain goats in one of the most beautiful places on earth. Or maybe we could just sit in the sunshine like the couple next to us, holding hands and watching children play until we were old and gray.

Fuck, I was falling apart. And I knew what I was about to suggest was a gigantic risk. It might even ruin the rest of our time together. Kill the vibes. Shatter the perfect bubble we'd been living in. But I had to take the chance. I'd never forgive myself if I didn't.

"Do you..." I bit my cheek as my heart kicked at my ribs. "Should we exchange numbers? I'd like to maybe call you sometime. Away from here. When we're back home. Maybe we could even—"

"Darryn." My name, the way she said it, was a verbal stop sign, a hand on my chest pushing me back.

"Never mind." I rubbed my eyebrow while my heart reversed course and plummeted toward my stomach. "I get it."

"I just think—"

"No, it's okay." Whatever she was thinking, that I was feeling this more than she was, that she didn't want the complication of some difficult, long-distance reality after this perfect dream, that her phone might literally explode if she tried to add one more contact, I really couldn't hear it. "How's your drink?"

Accepting the change in topic, she stared down at her dark cherry-colored cocktail and replied, "It's, um, really delicious. It might even be the best drink I've ever had." She spun the glass over the table's weathered wood planks. "But I don't think it's the kind of drink I could order all the time. It would be too sweet. Too perfect." She looked up at me, and her eyes shone in the late afternoon sun. "I'd never want to drink anything else."

Okay, maybe she wasn't changing the topic. "And that would be bad?" I asked.

"Not bad," she said with a smile so pained it sent an arrow straight through my chest. "But it would be a problem. Because the bars where I live don't serve this drink. They don't have the ingredients. And maybe, as hard as I try to recreate it myself at home, it won't taste the same. I'll never get it right." Her chin wobbled. "And I'll spend the rest of my life wishing I'd just let this perfect drink at this perfect place under this perfect sky stay perfect. Just the way it was. Just the way it is."

She blinked a tear down her cheek, and I wanted to fall to my knees.

"Tell me you understand," she said as another tear fell. "Please."

"I do." In all honesty, I wasn't sure that I did. All I knew was that

I needed to make her stop crying, whatever it took. So I reached across the table, cupped her cheek, and brushed her tears away with my thumb. "It's okay."

Grasping my hand, she turned her head, kissed my palm, and whispered, "Thank you," against my skin.

I wished she didn't feel that way. I wished she was open to trying...I didn't even know what with me. Which was likely the problem with the drink in her metaphor. Aside from being in her hand all the time, it didn't really know what it wanted or how to make it happen.

But I wasn't a drink. I was a man who believed we could figure it out. I was a man who could be relentless when he wanted to be. And I still had some tricks up my sleeve.

So I pulled myself together, and while we had another round, while we devoured the burgers and fries we ordered an hour later, we listened to each other tell our best stories and share more of our lives until the sun started to set. And when the solar-powered string lights winding through the trees flickered on and raucous fiddle music filled the air, we moved to the back patio with at least half the population of Balsam Ridge to watch the bluegrass band that had started playing.

And then we danced.

We danced with each other. We danced with strangers who didn't feel like strangers. We danced with the older couple we'd been sitting next to. And when the woman asked me how long Hannah and I had been together, and I answered, "Two days," she laughed like it was the most wonderful thing she'd ever heard. We danced under the stars and the half-moon and the twinkly lights for hours, until I was pretty sure I had a blister on my big toe.

And, yeah, there was magic in this place. I was a believer now. And with the way Hannah's eyes glowed, her life-affirming squeal when I picked her up, spun her around, and kissed her deeply, I knew she believed it too. I just had to find a way to convince her that we could take the magic back to the real world with us.

Eventually, Hannah reminded me that Joey needed his dinner, so I dropped a twenty into the tip jar for the band. We waved goodbye to all the new friends we'd met and made our way back to the cabin.

And now, after I'd let Joey out, fed him, and then gone down on Hannah while she was spread out on the kitchen counter before fucking her there, I had her curled up next to me in the hammock. We were both still naked, both warm and heavy-limbed as the fire popped and crackled behind us.

Pointing up at a bright star hovering just below the moon, she asked, "What's that one?"

"Sirius." I kissed her head while we swung gently from side to side. Her leg was hooked over mine, her fingers toying with my chest hair while mine curled over her bare hip. I'd never felt so content.

After Joey trotted by again, dropped his tennis ball at my side, and I tossed it for him, she pointed at three stars slanting across the sky and asked, "And those?"

"Cygnus. Part of his wings." She followed my finger while I traced the rest of the constellation. "Cygnus is a swan."

Propping her chin on my chest, she looked up at me with her beautiful brown eyes and said, "Now I get why you chose Cassiopeia as your safe word. Be honest, you learned about the stars just to impress girls, right?"

I grinned down at her, said, "Is there any other reason?" Then I kissed her forehead. She nestled back against my chest, and while we fell into a comfortable, spent silence, the night sky opened up above us, stars arriving in layers upon layers in a darkness only afforded by the absence of electricity.

The river of the Milky Way flowed as freckles of light that had traveled over distances and lengths of time I could never fully wrap my head around came into view. And even though the moment—swaying in the hammock, her body molded to mine like we were puzzle pieces made to interlock—was temporary, insignificant in the vast expanse of the universe unfolding above us, nothing about it felt accidental.

I'd met her on purpose. We'd been booked at this cabin at the same time on purpose. We were staring up at these stars on this night on purpose. That had to mean something. And I knew she was scared. I knew that there were real life things making any decisions about a future together feel hard and scary. But I couldn't help but wonder, what if...

"I'm going to miss you," she said, maybe thinking about tomorrow morning too, about saying goodbye.

Pulling her closer, I said, "I'm going to miss you too," even while my brain churned through a dozen possible scenarios where I wouldn't have to miss her. Maybe I could move to Sequim. There had to be a VA near there. Maybe I could transfer. But what about my house? Jeremiah's home base? My parents who weren't getting any younger?

Okay, maybe we could just swap weekends. I'd visit her, or she could visit me, or we could go somewhere entirely new with each other. But we probably wouldn't be able to do that every weekend, not with our jobs and our lives and our responsibilities. And, of course, money. So we could do every other weekend. Or maybe once a month.

A hollow emptiness churned in my stomach, because as soon as the thought hit me, I knew once a month wouldn't be enough. Not even close. We'd spend so much time missing each other.

The night was mild. The fire was warm. Her body was even warmer. And the cold mist sinking into my bones, the stress and worry tightening my shoulders and clenching my jaw, felt as out of place up here as a six-lane-highway traffic jam.

And maybe that's what she'd meant at the saloon. Maybe we couldn't recreate this cocktail. Maybe a chance and unlikely connection like ours would only collapse under the weight of our real-world lives. Maybe what we had together only existed here, in this place, with the stars and the magic and the fire. Because she was like that fire for me, burning bright and hot and perfect. And something inside me broke when I imagined watching that fire fade away no matter how hard we tried to keep it lit.

So maybe she was right. Maybe this was it for us for now. And maybe I needed to stop trying to figure out the future and just be grateful to be with her in the present. Even if our present would only last a little while longer.

CHAPTER TWELVE

HANNAH

I DIDN'T KNOW what time it was, but it was dark, and I hoped morning was still far away.

He'd woken me up with kisses. Kisses on my lips, my neck, my throat while he rolled me onto my back and held my hands above my head. Kisses between my legs while my fingers dove into his hair.

He whispered things to me, some of it I could hear, some I couldn't. He told me that I was soft and warm and beautiful. That he loved my breasts, my belly, my thighs. He rolled me onto my side again, bent my knee up, and pushed into me from behind. And while his hand gripped my thigh before slipping between my legs, I wondered if I was dreaming. Just like the first time we were together, like every time in between.

"I love this," he said against my neck in the quiet darkness of our room. "I love how you feel. I love your body. I love being inside you. I love making love to you."

"I love making love to you too," I told him, sighing when he rested his lips on my shoulder, his breath warm against my skin.

And it felt like we were saying more to each other, admitting more. But then we grew quiet, focused, and I let myself drown in him until his fingers between my legs pushed me back up to the surface. Until I whispered his name as I fractured into a thousand particles of heat and light, a new constellation only he could see.

And afterward, after he held his breath and tensed and came almost silently, while he was still inside me, still holding me in his arms, I tried to stay awake. I tried to keep my eyes open and savor every last minute with him as he kissed my shoulder and whispered something I could almost hear. Something so sweet and true.

But when I opened my eyes again, sunlight streamed through the windows, the bed was empty, and the smell of bacon and fresh coffee rose to greet me for the last time.

"No great big goodbyes." I clung to him in front of my rental car, wishing I never had to let go. "Please."

Wrapping me up even more tightly in his arms, he kissed my head and said, "Okay." His voice was thick, and it made my eyes burn. "No great big goodbyes."

When Joey stood to rest his paws on my knee, I pulled out of Darryn's arms, picked the dog up, and kissed his furry little face. "No great big goodbyes from you either." I passed Darryn his dog while tears streaked down my cheeks.

"Sweetheart, don't cry." He brushed my cheeks dry. "Are you sure you don't want to—"

I cut him off with a kiss, soft and lingering and tasting like salt from the tears he hadn't been able to catch. "It was perfect," I said. Then I stared up at him, pleading silently. *Let's give each other this one perfect thing we can carry with us for the rest of our lives.*

His chin ducked into a small nod, then his lips hitched. "But you know where I am if you change your mind."

He'd snuck his business card into my pants pocket, hoping I wouldn't notice until I'd left. But I'd felt it right away, like a warm stone against my thigh.

"I know," I said, trying to smile back but having a hard time pulling it off.

"Can I take a picture of us at least? Just one?"

I'd forgotten to charge it last night, so my phone was dead. And he didn't have my number, so I'd never get a copy of it. But he would. He'd have proof that the weekend had happened. It seemed important that at least one piece of physical evidence of our time together would exist in the world outside of Balsam Ridge. So I said, "Of course."

Setting Joey down, Darryn tossed him his ball. Then he hauled me into his arms. "Thank you, Hannah. This weekend was actually magic."

While pressure built behind my eyes, I said, "You mostly mean the orgasms, right?"

He laughed and kissed my head, then angled us toward his phone. And I don't know how many pictures he took. All I knew was that it was definitely more than one. I also knew that if I didn't leave the comfort of his arms right then, I might never leave it at all. Even though he was going to stay a bit longer to clean up and "do some other things," I had to go. I had a rental car to return, a plane to catch, and one day of travel to figure out how to go to work and talk to people and live a normal life again. Without him.

He lowered his phone, and I kissed him, letting him pick me up clear off the ground as he kissed me back so deeply and thoroughly I could barely breathe. When he set me down, I placed my hand over his heart and said, "This. You. This weekend. It's a top ten-er."

"Are you kidding?" Cradling my face, he held my stare. "Hannah James, you're in my top three."

Something inside my chest cracked in half, but somehow, after he gave me one last kiss, I stepped away from him on wobbly legs, turned around, and got into my car.

This time when I drove away, while he stood on the porch with Joey sitting beside him, while he waved at me with one hand and ran a knuckle under his eye with the other, I did it smiling. Crying, but smiling.

CHAPTER THIRTEEN

DARRYN

So THIS IS what heartbreak feels like.

Remember when I said that Hannah had been right? That what we had would be too hard to keep going once we got home? That being without her was better than trying to be with her and risking that it might all fall apart?

Yeah, well, I was wrong. Dead wrong.

I was worthless without her. Miserable. All day. All night. At home. In my car. At work. I mean, my poor clients. But it was really fucking hard to take care of other people's unmet needs when mine were screaming at me in surround sound twenty-four hours a day.

I was even a disaster at my folks' house last night. It wasn't my fault. I had fully planned on faking my way through family dinner without anyone knowing how deeply I was drowning. But my mom made her pea and prosciutto pasta, the same meal I'd made for Hannah at the cabin, and I couldn't eat a bite. Which I'm pretty sure scared the shit out of both my parents, because if there was one thing I could be counted on to do even if the world was about to end, it was eat.

Joke's on me I guess, because missing Hannah was worse than the world ending.

It had been two weeks since I watched her drive away from me, and I couldn't get past it. No matter how hard I tried, I couldn't get past her. She was everywhere. I couldn't listen to my cowboy music playlist anymore. Couldn't look up at the stars. Could barely take a breath without a sharp pain boring into my side. I'd heard the saying before, missing someone so much you couldn't breathe, but I always figured it was metaphorical. I didn't realize it was actually a knife between the ribs, twisting, digging a little deeper with every day she didn't pick up my card and call me. Every day I spent doing this, lying sprawled out on my bed with Joey snoring beside me, watching the light shift across my ceiling until I finally fell asleep.

My phone buzzed, Joey's head whipped up, and my heart lurched into my throat. Every phone call sent a painful jolt of hope through me. What if it was her this time? What if she'd finally decided, *You know what? Fuck it. Let's do this.*

"Sorry, bud." I scratched Joey behind his ear after noticing the caller ID. "Not this time." While he grumbled, curling into a tight little bean, I accepted the call. "Hey, Mattie."

"Darryn, what's wrong with you?"

Staring up at my listlessly circling ceiling fan, I lied, "Nothing."

"Really? Because Mom just called me. She said you didn't eat anything at dinner last night and that you looked like you got run over by a truck. What happened? Is it something with J?"

I sat up, grounding the heel of my palm into my eye while Joey grumbled again and repositioned himself between my legs. "No. Jeremiah's good. He's great, actually. Just got a raise."

"Oh, nice," Mattie said. "Good for him."

"Yeah." I could hear it in my voice, the defeat, the despair, and I knew he'd hear it too. After working with the men at his sober living home for over a decade, nothing got by Mattie.

"All right, Darryn."

Shit. Here we go.

"I just saw you a few weeks ago, and you were fine. Now you're obviously not. What's wrong? Talk to me."

Closing my eyes, accepting my fate, I told him, "I met someone."

"Really? It's about time. That's great."

"It was," I agreed while my throat closed up. "It was really great."

"Was?" he asked.

"Yeah. It's over now."

"Darryn, you were *just* here. How the hell is it over already? Did you meet her before you came to visit?"

Over the next few sad and depressing minutes, I told my big brother everything. I told him about the double-booking, about the rain and the puzzle and the stars and the sinking suspicion that I'd accidentally fallen in love with a stranger who made me feel like I'd known her my entire life. Then I told him about how she'd driven away and hadn't looked back. Or maybe she had. Maybe she'd checked us out in her rearview. She'd been wearing sunglasses, so it was hard to tell.

"Wait," Mattie said. "You don't even have her number?"

My shoulders sank. "No. I gave her my card, and she hasn't called. So I think that's probably that. I should just be happy it happened at all. Most people go their whole lives without an experience like the one I had with Hannah. Better to have loved and lost, or whatever they say."

"Loved? Hmm." It was a thoughtful hum, deliberate, concerning. "I think we need someone else's input here. Hang on."

My eyes flared. "Mattie, what are you doing?" Only silence responded. "Wait, you're not fucking calling Dad, are you?"

"I'll be your daddy, if you want."

Palming my forehead at the familiar voice joining the call, I said, "Hi, Cole."

"What's up, big D?" Cole Sanderson—the Makers' drummer and my brother's best friend—asked. "Mad said you needed help."

"He met a woman," Mattie said.

"That's great, man. It's about time," Cole echoed, making me realize that apparently I'd been single for a noticeable length of time. "So what's the problem?"

"The problem, Cole," Mattie said to the man who was essentially my second oldest brother, "is that she lives in another city and doesn't think they could work long-distance."

"Ha." Cole chuckled. "I know all too well about *that* little wrinkle."

"That's why I looped you in," Mattie said. "Thought you might have some words of wisdom."

"Oh, right." I sat up a little straighter. "You and Mira, you two were long-distance for a while." Cole had met Mira before Mattie and Ashley's wedding. He'd agreed to be her fake date to help her save face in front of her ex, and then they became involved even though he lived in Seattle, and she lived in Red Falls.

"We were," he muttered. "It sucked. Do not recommend."

Slumping again, I said, "I think that's why Hannah doesn't even want to try. Or maybe it's just me. Maybe I read the whole weekend all wrong."

"Weekend?" Cole asked, and I told him the whole story again while Mattie listened.

"Wow," Cole said once I was finished. "I mean..."

"I know," Mattie said.

"I see why you called me," Cole added.

"You get it, right?" Mattie asked.

And when Cole answered, "Totally," I broke.

"Would you two mind telling me what the hell you're talking about?"

"Hang on," Cole said, then he called out, "Hey, sugar, you have a minute?"

"Wait, Cole," I tried to interject, not necessarily wanting every single person in the small town of Red Falls to know my love life woes. But it was too late.

"You're on speaker with Mira now," Cole said. "So keep it classy."

"What's going on?" I heard Mira ask. She sounded wary but amused. Which was kind of the vibe Cole brought to every function, so she was probably used to it.

Listening with an exhausted acceptance while Cole and Mattie filled Mira in, I wondered briefly how my afternoon had gone so far off the rails.

"Oh, Darryn," Mira said. "I'm sorry. She sounds amazing."

I'd only met Mira twice: once at the wedding, and again a few weeks ago when we picked Cole up from her bakery for a guys' night out during my visit. But I didn't need to spend more time with her to know that she was a total sweetheart. And perfect for Cole.

"Thanks, Mira," I said glumly.

"Sugar, do you remember when you felt the same way as Hannah?" Cole asked Mira. "When I told you I wanted to move here, and you panicked, said no, then gave me a cupcake for my drive back to Seattle before shoving me out into the rain?"

"Wait. What?" This pulled me up short. "You gave him a cupcake?"

Mira groaned. "I'm never living that down, am I?"

"It's like I tell the guys," Mattie replied, giving her shit, "our pasts don't define us, but they do follow us wherever we go."

"Look," Mira groused. "I was terrified, and Cole was a mess. If you're going to tell a woman that you want to upheave your entire life for her, maybe don't do it when you haven't slept for three days and look like you're on the edge of a nervous breakdown."

"That's fair," Cole said, and then there was a muffled, smacking sound, like maybe they'd kissed. Which made my chest ache.

"So what do I do?" I rubbed my sternum while Joey stared up at me with his big, sweet eyes. "How do I convince her to give me a chance?"

"Do you know what she's worried about?" Mira asked. "Like, specifically?"

I'd been thinking about that a lot over the last two weeks. And I'd realized that while there were probably a lot of factors involved in her decision to end it at the cabin, I thought that the biggest one was timing.

"Her son had just left for college before we met, and it was really rough for her. That's why she'd come to Balsam Ridge in the first place, because being home without him was too hard. So I think she wasn't interested in another thing that might hurt her. Like, she didn't want another goodbye, in case it didn't work out with us. She didn't want something that might end up making her feel even more alone."

"That makes so much sense," Mira said. "I swear, when Ian goes off to college, I'm going to be an absolute disaster." Her voice warbled. "I can't even think about it without..."

"Oh, sugar," Cole said when Mira trailed off. "Come here. It'll be okay."

I assumed there was probably a hug on their side of the call, maybe another kiss. The ache in my chest intensified.

"Okay, so maybe she just needs more time," Mattie suggested.

"Yeah." Mira's voice was watery. "Maybe it was just too soon, and she was too emotionally raw to think about the future. Maybe she's feeling differently now. Because I'm sure she misses you too. I'm sure she's pacing around her house wondering if she made the right choice. She's probably wishing she'd handled things differently. Maybe she has some regrets. Like that stupid cupcake," she said under her breath.

"If she does have regrets," I said, not entirely convinced, "how long should I wait to find out? How long would it take after a kid goes off to college for their mom to be ready to consider a long-distance relationship with someone she's only spent a couple of days with?" Silence followed my question. "Anyone?" I asked.

"Bueller?" Cole quipped.

"Cole, no," Mattie said. "You have *got* to stop using that joke."

"Why? It's a classic."

Mattie scoffed. "It's a dinosaur."

"I don't know, Darryn," Mira said, ignoring their bickering. "I don't know how long it would take."

"But I know someone who does," Mattie said before calling out, "Ashley, you around?"

I palmed my forehead. Was this what it had come to? I needed an army of friends and family to help me with my nonexistent love life?

"Putting you on speaker," Mattie said. Then a voice that definitely wasn't Ashley's asked, "What's going on in here?"

"Hey, Maude Alice," Mattie said. "Darryn's on the line. He's having romance problems."

"Impossible," Ashley's mom said. "Darryn is the best looking of all you Madigan boys. And the sweetest too."

"Why, thank you," I said smugly while Mattie chirped, "Are you kidding me right now?"

"Did you need me?" *That* was Ashley, the love of Mattie's life. They'd only met ten months ago, and it was wild to think that there was a time when they weren't together. In fact, Mattie, Cole, and I had that in common: we were all middle-aged men who hadn't found "the one" until our 40s and 50s. At least they got to be with their "one."

"Hey, Ashley," Mira said while I ran my fingers over Joey's wiry tail "We still need that girls' night."

"Hi, Mira. We do." Ashley sounded closer now. "Does Thursday work?"

"I'm with Mom on Thursday. But I'm free Friday."

"It's a date," Ashley said. Then, after a beat, "Why are we on speaker phone?"

"Because of me," I said miserably. My ear was starting to sweat, so I put my phone on speaker too. "Welcome to my super sad romance intervention."

"Darryn?" Ashley asked. "Is that you?"

"We need your help with something," Mattie told her, and after I gave Ashley and everyone else the rundown, *again*, I realized that it didn't hurt quite as badly that time. Maybe, if I told every person I'd ever met our story, I could just talk my feelings for Hannah down to a tolerable level. Like some kind of heartbreak exposure therapy.

"Wow," Ashley said once I was finished, and I couldn't tell if it was a good wow or a bad one.

I was about to ask her when Maude Alice said, "This Hannah person is obviously just confused. Because you are a catch, Darryn Madigan. If I wasn't over twenty years older than you and in my own situationship, I'd be—"

"Mother, please," Ashley said. "Overshare."

That made me laugh, at least.

"Okay, Darryn." Ashley shifted into business mode. "It sounds like you and Hannah shared something truly special. Right people, but meeting at the wrong time. And considering how inconsolable I was when Davis went off to college, I—"

"You were inconsolable? Mom, you never told me that."

"Is that Davis?" I asked when a new voice that sounded just like Ashley's joined the call, making this a seven-person conversation now, and officially ridiculous.

"Yeah," Davis, Ashley's daughter, said. "Who's this?"

"It's Darryn, honey," Ashley explained. "He's having love life problems."

"That is highly relatable," Davis said under her breath, then, louder, "Hi, Darryn."

"Hi, Davis. Everything still going good with you?" Davis and her boyfriend Kev had just gotten back together after a long and painful separation when I'd visited.

"Everything is amazing," she said, and the smile in her voice was undeniable. "But what's up with you?"

Thankfully, Ashley saved me from having to spill my bruised guts again by catching Davis up.

"Oh no," Davis said, sounding genuinely distraught. "What are you gonna do?"

"I have no idea," I replied.

"That's why we're all here," Cole said. "It takes a village."

"Apparently," I agreed miserably.

Joey's ear twitched while he grunted his agreement.

"Was that Joey?" Mattie asked.

"Yep."

In a mushy voice that perked Joey's head back up, Mattie said, "How's my wittle guy?"

"He's good." I sniffed while Joey gave his tail a lethargic wag. "A little sad, though. I think he misses her too."

At least five separate voices came together in a chorus of *aws*.

"Okay, we need to figure this out right now," Mattie said. "Murphy will never forgive me if I let his favorite dog friend be sad."

As if on cue, a low bark rumbled across the line.

"Don't worry, Murph," Mattie said to their giant Saint Bernard. "We'll get this sorted out."

Smiling weakly, I scratched Joey's head again, then asked, "Ashley, how long did it take after Davis left before you started to feel better? How long before you might have wanted to, say, go on a date with someone new?" *Someone who lives two hours away and might complicate your life in ways you're not interested in?*

"It took a while," Ashley said. "Before she left, Davis gave me this blanket that was a collage of pictures of her growing up. I wore it like a cape for a week at least."

"Oh, Mom," Davis said. "That's so sweet."

"It was a tragedy," Maude Alice cut in dryly. "Your mom *and* that blanket were both in shambles."

"Anyway," Ashley said, and I could practically hear her side-eyeing her mother. "I think I started feeling like a human being again after a couple of weeks. Maybe a month."

"I'm taking notes," Mira said. "I'm gonna tell Ian he needs to get me one of those blankets before he goes anywhere."

"Ask him to get one for me too," Cole requested.

"So, two weeks to a month?" I repeated for clarity. "Because it's already been two weeks, so maybe I should wait another two?" Could I wait another two weeks? It was only fourteen days. Half a month. A single pay period. But it seemed impossible.

"It depends," Cole said. "What are you planning? How are you going to reach out to her?"

"I haven't really planned anything," I admitted. "I don't have her number or her address."

"What's her last name?" Davis asked. "You said she lives in Sequim?"

"James. And yeah. She's a high school counselor there."

"Yes, that's good info. Hang on." Ten seconds later, Davis said, "Found her. Wow, Darryn. She's gorgeous."

"You found her?" My toes started to tingle. "And there's a picture?"

"Yep. Right there on the front page of her high school's website. She won some kind of best counselor award last year. Seems like a pretty big deal. Have you honestly never googled her?"

"No," I said, wondering why I hadn't, but knowing that was certainly how I'd be spending the rest of my day.

"Men," Davis sighed. "So silly."

"Okay, so we have an address for her now," Mattie said. "That's a start."

"I can't just go over there, though, right? I can't walk into a high school and be like 'Hi, Hannah. Remember me? Cuz I think I'm in love with you.'"

"Oh my god," Davis cooed. Or maybe it was Ashley. It was hard to tell with those two.

"Yeah, that's not a good idea," Cole said, staying grounded. "Because she's probably skittish. And coming in hot like that might scare her off even more."

After a quiet, thoughtful moment, another new voice said, "Uh, hey, guys. Is everything okay? I just came up to see if Davis wanted to grab some lunch, but this situation seems...kinda intense."

"It's Kev," Davis explained. "Come in, babe. We're on a conference call with Mira and Cole trying to help Darryn out with some girl trouble."

Davis was astonishingly efficient in describing the situation to

Kev, who was one of the men staying at Mattie's sober living home. Once she was finished, he said, "Oh, man. This is wild, but I've seen it before. Loads of times."

"You have?" I frowned skeptically at the phone, and at the twenty-something youngster speaking to me through it.

"Well, not in real life," he explained. "But it's, like, romance novel 101. Forced proximity, a life-changing vacation fling, catching big feelings but there's all this real-world aftermath."

"You're right," Ashley said brightly. "This is just like *The Hound's Secret Mate*."

"The hound's what?" I asked.

"Kev and Mom read the same romance books," Davis said. "And yeah, it's as awkward for me as it sounds."

"But they made it work?" Hope stirred beneath my ribs. "The hound and his secret mate?"

"Of course," Kev and Ashley answered in unison.

"How?" I pleaded. "What do I do?"

"Okay," Kev said. "Let me think." There was a series of *pop*s, like he'd cracked his knuckles. "First of all, we need to figure out her backstory. Because backstory is everything. It's her motivation, her fear, all that stuff. It's why she feels like not being with you is safer than trying."

"She said she'd been divorced, and he'd cheated."

"Eesh," Kev said. "Yeah, that would make it hard to trust again. Anything else? Anything she might be afraid of? Any pressures she's under?"

For some reason, the conversation we had at the saloon about her call with William popped into my mind. "She'd talked to her kid when we were up there. And after, she was really distant. So I asked her about it, and apparently one of his friends had been upset because his parents were selling the house he'd grown up in. He felt like they were taking his room. And I get that, because I feel that way about Jeremiah's room too. Like if I ever decided to move, it would be really hard..."

The words died on my tongue as it all crashed into me at once.

"Oh," Ashley said, like it might have crashed into her too. "I get it now."

"So maybe she was already thinking about the future," Kev said. "Maybe, in her mind, she'd already put the for-sale sign up in her yard. Which is great, because it means she's really into you and might have considered moving for you. But also not great, because—"

"She sees being with me as something that will potentially upset her kid."

"Jeez," Cole said. "Why does everything have to be so complicated at our age?"

"We've all lived too much life to make sharing it with someone else easy," Mattie answered.

"Don't lose hope yet," Kev said. "In romance novels, everyone gets their happily ever after, no matter how old they are or how much life they've lived. So you want to reach out to her again, but you need to be careful about it. You need to meet her where she is, but also let her know that you're all in. You need to leave no doubt in her mind that you'll do whatever it takes to be with her. Even if it means waiting patiently for her to be ready. Even if it means just being friends at first. Whatever she needs, you gotta be willing to do it with your whole chest." He took a slow, thoughtful breath, let it out, then said, "I think what we need here is a grand gesture."

"Yes," Davis said softly, and I wondered if she was looking directly at Kev. "Sometimes we need to be swept off our feet."

"A grand gesture?" I tugged on my lower lip. "What, like skywriting or hiring a mariachi band or something?"

"No. I mean, those *are* grand gestures. But they won't work here." While Kev spoke, everyone else went completely silent, like students recognizing that class was in session. "A grand gesture doesn't need to be big or flashy. In fact, the best ones usually aren't. A good grand gesture should make Hannah feel seen and understood. It should be meaningful to her. And, in this case, I think it needs to be easy, something that doesn't put any pressure on her. Something that says 'This is how much I care about you, or how much I miss you. This is what you mean to me. But it's not a demand on you to respond. It's only… an invitation.'"

There was a spark, a flame, and then a fire lit me up from the inside. Leaping off my bed, I shot to my feet and said, "I've got it. I know exactly what to do."

"Of course you do, dear," Maude Alice said.

"That's the spirit," Cole cheered.

"How much of this can I tell Mom?" Mattie asked. "Because you know she's going to check back in."

"I'll call her," I said. My heart was beating so hard and fast I wondered if it would bust straight out of my chest. "Thank you, everyone. Especially you, Kev. I think I'm gonna need your number on speed dial."

"Anytime, man," Kev said. "Happy to help."

"You'd better keep us posted," Davis warned. "I will not be chill about this until I know how it turns out."

"Okay, I will. You're the best. All of you."

After Cole's lighthearted "like I said, it takes a village," we said our goodbyes, I ended the call, and I got to work.

CHAPTER FOURTEEN

HANNAH

ONE WEEK LATER

"How's it going?" Steph asked, perched on the corner of my desk in her gray pencil skirt and canary yellow cardigan sweater, repeating the same question she'd been asking me every day for the last three weeks.

"Fine," I said, repeating the same answer.

"Then maybe you should tell that to your face."

I gave her a look.

"What? It's been three weeks, Hannah. And you're still barely human."

I shrugged. Only one shoulder. Lifting them both at once was too hard.

"Are you ever going to call him?"

"I don't know."

It was one of the things I'd been asking myself on repeat since I got back from the cabin. Along with other gems like: Why did you let him go? Why do you spend every night in your bed staring at his business card before you eventually fall asleep lonely and missing him, only to wake up lonelier and missing him even more? What are you afraid of? What is wrong with you?

And the worst part was, I didn't have an answer for any of them. In Balsam Ridge, it had all seemed so clear. Darryn and I couldn't work in the real world. We were meant to exist there, not here. The magic lived there. It didn't live here. But I must have been wrong, because these days, *I* was barely existing here. William had even started to worry about me.

Studying her nails, Steph asked, "So are you stalking his social media like a psychopath or what?"

"He's not on social media." I clicked *send* on an email to a parent who wanted to switch her kid's biology class to third period. "I checked."

"Of course he isn't." She sighed deeply, her copper curls sliding over her shoulders. "The great ones never are."

"Hey, Steph." I closed my laptop so I could give her my full attention. "I know I've been a mess lately. I know it might not seem like it was a good trip for me. But it was. It really was." *Do not cry, Hannah. Hold it together.* "It was perfect."

Her expression was uncharacteristically soft as she reached down to squeeze my hand. "I know it was."

Squeezing her back, I wondered why a soft expression from someone who didn't normally pass them out hit so hard, like an emotional wallop. But what I'd said was true. Even though I missed Darryn so much, I spent more time staring blankly at my walls than when I had mono at ten years old, being in that cabin, being with him, had helped me. It had let me come back to my empty house with a less empty heart. "Thank you for setting it up for me."

"You're welcome, babe. But don't expect the same results next time." She hopped off my desk. "That shit was kismet. And I still think you should drive to Olympia, find that man, and live happily ever after. But"—she picked a fleck of lint off her sweater—"what do I know. Oh, and this is for you. Came to my box by accident."

The envelope she set on my desk was made out to Hannah James at North Lark High School. There was no return address.

"Wanna get lunch with me later?" she asked while I picked up the envelope.

"Sure." I studied the handwriting, my name written in tidy block letters. "Sounds good," I said, and I wasn't sure why, but I waited until she closed the door before I opened it.

Reaching inside, I pulled out a handwritten letter. It was short and sweet, and I could barely read it through the sudden tears clouding my vision.

> *Dear Hannah,*
>
> *Maybe I shouldn't have, but after you left me at the cabin, I drove back to the saloon and begged them for the recipe for your cocktail. I know it was a metaphor, but the thing is, I think we were wrong. I think the drink tastes just as good out here as it did there. Maybe even better. If you want to try it out, I'd love to make one for you. I don't know what your plans are next weekend, but if you're free, I have it on good authority that this place is notorious for double-booking their guests.*
>
> *All my love,*
> *Darryn*
> *P.S. I miss you so fucking much.*

The next page of the letter was a rental listing for a cottage at a vineyard located halfway between Sequim and Olympia. There was a phone number scrawled across the top along with the note: *This one has running water. And a hot tub ;) Call me. Please.*

Snatching my phone off my desk so fast it flew out of my hands and clattered onto the floor, I hissed a curse, picked it up, and punched in his number.

The second his smooth, deep voice brushed across my ear, my

breath caught, my heart stopped, and then I blurted out, "I miss you so fucking much too. Every day, I miss you. Every night. Every time I look up at the stars, my heart feels like it's breaking. And I *was* wrong, Darryn. Because one weekend with you wasn't enough. One top ten moment with you wasn't enough. I want more. I want whatever I can get. However I can get it. And I'm so sorry I didn't realize it sooner."

"Hannah, sweetheart." Hearing him again was like sitting next to a fire after spending three weeks out in the snow. "There is nothing to be sorry for."

"There is, though." I swiped hot, fat tears from my cheeks. "I should have been braver. I should have been honest. I should have told you, at the very least, that meeting you was one of the best things that has ever happened to me."

"God," he said, "I've been a mess without you."

Clutching my phone to my chest, holding it over my wildly beating heart before raising it back to my ear, I asked for the one thing I hadn't been able to stop thinking about. "Will you send me the picture? The one you took of us?"

"I think I took about fifteen. But yes, of course. Hang on."

I stared at my screen, my fingers trembling. And then, there it was. He'd framed us well, with the mountains rising behind us and the morning sun glinting in our eyes. Seeing him again, finally seeing him again, seeing *us* together, both smiling but also so obviously on the verge of tears, I could barely hold myself together. But it was the next picture he sent that took me apart piece by piece.

"Darryn, is that?"

"Our puzzle," he said. "I kinda stole it. I sent PeePaw a new one, I promise. But I brought ours home and put it back together. Then I framed it. It's hanging over my bed now and—Shit, Hannah. Are you crying?"

"Yes," I blubbered. "Yes, I'm crying. You... You have our puzzle."

"I also took one of the mugs you used, and a fork you'd eaten with, and the pillowcase you slept on. I had a lot of explaining to do, but PeePaw was cool about it. I think he's rooting for us."

Through my tears, I managed to say, "Before I drove out of town, I stopped by the General and bought that Montana wildflowers book you'd been looking at. I keep it on my nightstand."

"Really?" I didn't need to see him to know he was smiling.

"Sometimes I just hold it. Just put my fingers over where you'd put yours and try to feel you."

"Will you come to the cottage with me this weekend?" he asked. "No pressure, I promise. I just need to see you. I need to feel you and touch you and kiss you. God, Hannah. I need to kiss you again like I need air."

I didn't tell him that I needed to kiss him too. I didn't tell him that maybe I wanted some pressure. I only told him the single word flashing through my mind and my heart in bright, glittery, neon letters: "Yes."

EPILOGUE
SIX MONTHS LATER

THIS HAD BEEN one of the best days of my life. A top three for sure.

We'd spent the morning cross-country skiing through soft spring snow in Olympic National Park and made love in our cute little rental all afternoon, and now I was sitting in a packed bar surrounded by cheering and smiling strangers. My drink was perfect, the vibes were immaculate, and my boyfriend was up on stage, his head tilted back and the microphone held high, his shirt riding up just enough to show a sliver of skin above his jeans as he absolutely demolished the final high note in Madonna's "Ray of Light."

Leaping to my feet as the outro pumped through the speakers, I bracketed my mouth with my hands and screamed so loud I wondered if I'd have any voice left in the morning. But I didn't care.

Six months ago, Darryn and I started sneaking away to different rentals almost every weekend. Four months ago, we started staying at each other's houses and meeting each other's families. And three months ago, we finally locked each other down and made our relationship official. He was my boyfriend. I was his girlfriend. And I loved him with a kind of all-encompassing desperation I'd never felt for any man before, let alone one I met in my forties. It really never was too late.

But we'd been living one weekend at a time for so long now, both of us spending way too much money on gas and VRBOs, that I couldn't even remember what my life had been like before Darryn. It was messy and a little chaotic, and even though we hadn't come up with a plan yet for how to be closer, live closer, share a life that didn't look like a never-ending string of wild adventures, I had never, ever been happier. Darryn never pressured me. I didn't pressure him. We just appreciated each other. And when he hopped off the stage to a roar of applause in this rowdy karaoke bar neither of us had ever been to before, I really wanted to *appreciate* him again.

He gave high fives and bumped fists on his way back to our table, but his eyes were on me, his lips quirking into that crooked smile that always made my belly flip.

When he reached me, I threw my arms around his neck and said, "That was so fucking hot," into his ear.

He growled and picked me up, and I wrapped my legs around his waist while I kissed him fiercely. "Incredible," I said, kissing his lips, his cheek, his neck. "I can't believe you made me wait six months for that."

"Yeah?" He set me down, smiling like a thousand-watt lightbulb. "I put some extra sauce on it tonight." He winked. "Just for you."

Pushing him down into his chair, I sat across his lap, and while a very inebriated man wearing a World's Best Grandpa hat got up to sing "No Diggity" of all things, I slid my hand up the front of Darryn's soft shirt, leaned in close, and said, "I want you to sing to me like that every night."

His arms closed around me, holding me tight as he kissed my neck, then asked, "Wanna get out of here?"

Leaning back, catching his hungry stare, I said, "Please."

He took my hand, and I followed behind him out of the bar while he high-fived and thanked more nice people waiting to praise his performance. And in that moment, somehow, impossibly, I fell even more deeply in love with him.

It happened all the time. Just when I thought I couldn't love him more, that my heart had hit its limit, he'd show me with an unexpected flower delivery at work or a sweet postcard in the mail or by sharing his private karaoke life with me, that maybe I didn't know how much I could love. Maybe my love for him was limitless.

I thought it would be scary, making this decision. I thought I'd feel conflicted or uncertain, even after talking about it with William. But while we walked the few blocks back to our rental, while he led me inside, while I waited for him to let Joey out, I'd never felt so certain about anything.

It was time.

When he came back inside and Joey scampered in behind him, curling up on his doggy bed by the fireplace, I watched Darryn take off his coat and hang it on the hook by the door. I watched him step out of his boots and line them up neatly on the mat. Then, when he finally looked at me, I winked, turned toward the bedroom, pulled my sweater over my head, and tossed it somewhere behind me.

"Hannah?"

Unhooking my bra, I slid the straps off my shoulders and let it dangle from my fingertips before dropping it to the floor.

"Fuck, baby," he growled, making my skin sizzle. "What are you doing to me?"

Turning toward the door to our bedroom, I glanced back at him over my shoulder. Then I unbuttoned and unzipped my jeans, and when he palmed himself through his, I grinned and stepped inside.

By the time he caught up to me, I was bent over, sliding my jeans down my legs, giving him a full view of my ass in the lacy black panties I'd bought just for this occasion, for this night, for him.

"Shit," he hissed. "Are those new? Wait, don't move." He pressed his hand between my shoulder blades, urging me back down when I tried to straighten. "Give me a sec."

With my jeans pooled around my feet, I sighed when he pressed his rigid length into me. Taking hold of my hip, he slid his other hand down my back until his fingers hooked into the thin waistband of my panties and pulled, just a little. Just enough to catch a glimpse.

"These are"—he rocked into me—"so hot." Letting go of my hip, he reached between my breasts and hauled me upright as his fingers traveled around the band of my panties to the front. And then he slipped inside.

My knees wobbled, and I reached back for him, grasping his neck as he palmed my breast and found my clit.

I gasped, closed my eyes, held on for dear life. And because he knew my body now almost as well as I knew it myself, he whispered, "You're close already," into my ear, sliding a long, thick finger inside me, pumping slowly in and out.

"Not...my fault," I managed. Because what was a girl supposed to do when her boyfriend serenaded her with Johnny Cash before bringing the house down with Madonna? "You looked so good up there I almost crawled onto the stage."

He hummed. "Should I make you come like this, with your jeans around your ankles and my hand down the front of your sexy little panties? Is that what you want?"

"Mm-hmm," I moaned, pressing my lips together as he kissed my neck and pinched my nipple.

He pulled out of me, and when his finger returned to my clit, it was wet and slippery and determined.

"Yes. Fuck. Oh god." I don't know what I said after that, maybe nothing, maybe I only gasped and writhed as his finger circled faster and his thumb flicked over my nipple, as my orgasm rose, crested, and broke over me. I shuddered. My legs shook. I might have even collapsed if he hadn't been holding me up.

"You're so beautiful when you come," he said, his whispered voice sending an aftershock rippling through me. "The most beautiful thing I've ever seen."

Regaining control of my body by degrees, I turned in his arms, rucked his shirt up, and helped him pull it over his head. And then I sank to my knees.

"Hannah," he whispered, gazing down at me reverently as I unbuttoned his jeans, unzipped his fly, and pulled his erection out.

I kissed the broad head of his hard and leaking cock, licked a bead of precum from his tip. And then I took him deeply into my mouth.

"Christ, sweetheart. That feels so good."

Glancing up at him through my lashes, at his flexing abs and heaving chest, his glazed-over eyes staring down at me, my heart swelled until it ached. And when he reached down to cup my cheek, that ache blossomed into a deep, sweet, tender bruise. Because love did that. It made your heart hurt, like there wasn't enough room and the muscle had to stretch and grow to hold it all.

"Too good," he gritted out. "Gotta stop." Backing out of my mouth, he helped me up to my feet. "I want to be inside you when I come."

I nodded, and he picked me up and carried me to the bed. When he climbed on top of me and tried to settle between my legs, I rolled him over. I needed to be on top tonight. I needed to set the pace. I needed to see his eyes closing and hear his sigh as I held him in place and slid down onto him.

"Fuck," he grunted, digging his fingers into my ass while I started to move. "You're so good to me."

I bent forward to kiss his throat, his chest. I swirled my tongue around his nipple, then the other one. I sucked on them, which he loved.

"So good," he said again, holding me down as he fucked up into me.

In this position, he hit the perfect spot inside me with every snap of his hips, and I was going to come again. Fast. But I had things to do. To say. So I sat back up, set my hands on his chest, and checked my pace.

"I have something to tell you," I said, riding him slow and steady.

"Okay." His eyes were at half-mast, his head tilted back. I wasn't sure he was really paying attention, so I slowed even more.

"Do you remember the first time we met?"

"Yes," he replied, and I could tell by the little groove appearing between his brows that he wanted me to move faster. "I'll never forget. Your beautiful brown eyes all wide with shock when I opened the door. The way you couldn't stop staring at my chest." While I blew out a laugh, his groove etched itself more deeply. "I remember how my heart sank when you drove away. I didn't even know you then, but I didn't want you to leave."

"What about when I came back?" I asked.

Giving me two mind-scrambling thrusts, he said, "When you were crying in the rain, and I wanted to tear the world down just to get you dry and warm and safe in my arms?"

Heat bloomed inside my chest. "What about when our weekend was over? When I left for good? Do you remember that?"

"I always remember when you leave." Loosening his grip on my hips, stilling his, he said, "Every weekend we have together. Every time we say goodbye, it hits me like a freight train. Watching you drive away or watching you stay while I drive away. Knowing I won't take a full breath until I see you again. Yeah, Hannah. I remember."

A stinging pressure built behind my eyes, but I kept my voice steady as I said, "We've said so many goodbyes to each other. I thought it would get easier, but it just keeps getting harder."

His eyes were locked on mine now, fully open and heavy with concern. "Hannah? What are you trying to say?"

Brushing my thumb over the groove between his brows, trying to smooth it out, I said, "I think it's too hard, saying goodbye to you over and over. I think we've done it enough, don't you?"

His throat worked through a swallow. "What do you mean?"

"I don't want to say goodbye to you anymore."

He sat up, still inside me, and his eyes searched my face in panicked darts. "You don't want this to be over, do you? I know it's not perfect. I know it's hard. But please. Please don't—"

"No." I shook my head. "No, Darryn. That's not what I mean."

"It's not?"

I placed my hand over his heart, which thundered under my palm. This wasn't going like it had gone in my head. "I am in love with you." I kissed him softly, sliding up and down his shaft once, twice, punctuating each roll of my hips with "madly, deeply, unbearably in love with you."

Bracing himself with one hand on the bed, he slid the other behind my back, holding me in place as he rocked up into me again, making my eyelids flutter. "I love you too. But what are you trying to say?"

This was it. This was where I risked it all. "I want more, Darryn. I want more than weekends with you. I want morning coffee and grocery shopping and doing laundry and cooking dinner. I want long walks and short drives and reading in silence beside you with Joey curled up in my lap. I want to wake up next to you every morning and fall asleep next to you every night. I want to pay bills together and do our taxes and get oil changes and shovel the snow on our sidewalk. I love our adventures, so much. But I want boring too. I want boring, mundane, everyday life with you."

He'd stopped moving. I wasn't entirely sure he was breathing. So I pushed him back down to the bed where he'd be safe and asked, "Do you remember that job that came open in Olympia last month?"

He blinked, and at least that was a sign of life. "You said it wasn't the right fit for you because it was a middle school."

"What if I told you that I changed my mind? What if I told you that I applied?"

He refroze.

"What if," I said, sliding up and down his length again, trying to thaw him out, "I told you that they offered me the job?"

"They... What?"

"They offered me the job." I repeated. "I—"

"Wait... Can we... Can we just..."

"Darryn?" He was trembling beneath me. "Are you okay?"

"Fuck." Covering his face with his hands as tears leaked down his temples, he pushed out a raw and broken "Cassiopeia."

I tilted my head, confused. *Cassio—*

"Shit," I said, remembering. Lifting myself off him, I sat on my heels at his side. We hadn't had to use them since our tickle fight in the cabin, *no* or *stop* being plenty for as kinky as we ever got, but Cassiopeia had been his safe word. He'd just used his safe word. For this conversation.

"I'm sorry," I said to his hands still covering his face. Then I glanced down at his erection, still red and wet and bobbing sadly toward his stomach. This *definitely* wasn't going like it had gone in my head. "I didn't mean to ruin everything."

"You didn't ruin anything." His voice was thick and muffled. "It's me. I just... I need a second."

So I waited, and while he struggled to pull himself together, his breath hitching, chest shuddering, I fell apart. He was crying for me, for *us*. Because he loved me as much as I loved him, and the relief and joy and rightness I'd felt when I found out I got the job, I wondered if that was all hitting him at once.

After a moment, he took a shaky breath, wiped his eyes, and said, "I'm okay. I'm good."

Reaching for him, I turned his face to mine. When he saw the tears standing in my eyes, he hauled me on top of him and wrapped me up inside his arms. And there, in the safest place I'd ever known, I said, "I probably shouldn't have brought this up while we were fucking."

Laughter rumbled through his chest, and I raised my head, putting us eye to eye. He brushed my cheeks dry and asked, "What about William?"

Darryn and I had talked about it several times over the last couple of months, if one of us would be willing to move to be closer to the other. He'd offered first, because that's just who he was. But VA jobs were surprisingly hard to come by, and he had family in Olympia—his parents and his other brothers, all of whom I adored. I still hadn't met his brother who lived in Montana, the infamous Madigan, but I was sure I'd adore him too.

I wanted to be with Darryn. It was all I thought about sometimes. But until recently, I wasn't sure that I could move. With William at school, all I had keeping me tied to Sequim was Steph and my job—even though Steph thought I was nuts not to have moved already and would probably pack my bags for me tonight if I asked her to. Still, I was scared of leaving. I was scared that William would react like his friend had to the news that his childhood home would go on the market. I didn't want that for him. I wanted him to be able to see his friends whenever he was on a break from school. I wanted him to know he had a safe and comfortable home base to return to. I didn't want my choices to disrupt his life. Turns out, I shouldn't have worried.

"Funny thing about kids," I said. "Sometimes you just need to ask them how they feel about something."

"What did he say?"

"First, he said congratulations, and that he thinks you're the best. Then I asked him about his friend from the beach trip because he'd seemed so upset that his parents were moving. And he laughed at me. He said I'd gotten it wrong. He'd been annoyed because he thought his friend had been overreacting that day and was being unfair. He doesn't think that parents should have to stay stuck in place once their kids have moved out. Then he said he didn't care about his room, and that he'd find a way to see his friends. He just wants me to be happy."

"Of course he does." Darryn tucked a loose strand of my hair behind my ear. "He's a great kid. Even if he laughed at you, which wasn't very nice."

"I know, right?"

"So, um," he said, his expression cautious but hopeful, "are you going to take the job?"

"That depends." Fighting back another swell of tears, I asked, "Would it be okay if I moved in with you? I know it's a lot to ask, and I know you'll want to clear it with Joey and Jeremiah first, and I can find a place of my own in Olympia if you don't want—Hey!" I squealed when he rolled me over, pushed back inside me with one slow thrust, and said, "Fuck yes, you're moving in with me. Because I want things too. I want morning coffee and long walks too. I want fighting over the shower and doing puzzles at the dining room table. I want to send out obnoxious couple's Christmas cards every year wearing matching sweaters—Joey too. I want work parties and pizza nights and lazy sex and soft, slow kisses. I want summers camping and staring up at the stars. I want it all. Forever. With you."

Now it was my turn to cry during sex. "I love you," I said, over and over as I wrapped my arms and legs around him, as he found a rhythm, driving deeply into me. I said it again as we found release in each other, me first, Darryn close behind.

And when we were done, when he opened his eyes again and stared down at me, when my heart had to swell another inch to make room for everything I felt for him, he gave me one of those soft, slow kisses I couldn't wait to feel every single day and asked, "Should I rent the U-Haul now or...?"

My smile was watery, my chin wobbling. Until he kissed me again and said, "I love you too, Hannah. Thank you for showing up on PeePaw's porch. Thank you for being willing to spend the weekend with some random guy. Thank you for trusting me, for loving me." His lips quirked. "Thank you for letting me fuck you when you didn't even know my name."

Laughter bubbled up inside me.

"Thank you for everything," he said, and then we held each other, kissed each other, made love again once we were ready. And later, after we'd fallen asleep curled so tightly into each other I wasn't sure where I stopped and he began, I dreamed of him.

We were older. My hair was gray, so was his stubble. But his eyes were still piercingly blue. And while we swayed gently in a hammock under the stars, my hand on his chest, his wrapped around my hip while the Milky Way flowed above us, he pointed out the constellations shining in the night sky for me, and I thought, *what a magical life we've had.*

Thank you so much for reading Darryn and Hannah's story. If you'd like another Jess K Hardy novella that's completely free, visit jesskhardy.com.

ACKNOWLEDGMENTS

Sometimes you need to write a book that's just fun. And this book was fun. I knew the second that I gave Madigan brothers, the second I had them wandering around Madigan and Ashley's wedding in their tuxedos, that I wanted to write a story about one of them. And Darryn, the "usually most serious," brother according to Cole in Lips Like Sugar, was the guy.

I loved the idea of matching a high school counselor with someone who really could have used one when he was a teenager. Darryn lived through the worst years of Madigan's addiction not as a brother who could get upset and rage about it, but as their mother's shield, doing everything he could to make sure that she was protected and supported. Hannah is the first person who really validates him and the toll that took on him.

But this story isn't all fun. It touches on something my family is going through right now, sending a kid off to college. Last fall, my husband and I went camping. The lake we popped our tent by was stunning, the leaves on the trees were orange and golden, the weather was perfect, the stars were immaculate, and I was miserable. I couldn't figure out what was wrong with me. Until we started talking about our son leaving next year, and I sobbed for a solid thirty minutes. We only have one kid. We're a super tight family. And thinking of what our home will feel like without him in it, well, I had to write it out.

I hope you enjoyed this addition to the Bluebird Basin world, especially my favorite conference call ever, AKA Kev's Bromance

Book Club—and yes, I adore those books. If you haven't read them, please do. I had a fantastic time writing this book, and I hope you had a good time reading it too.

As always, I couldn't write without the support of my family, my husband and my son. I really couldn't have written this book without my son, so I'm especially grateful for him. Well, I'm always grateful for him.

Big thanks to my author friends who joined me in writing The Packing List, our later-in-life romance anthology where a shorter version of this story came to life. Thank you to Karen Booth, J. Calamy, Kate Canterbary, Michelle Donn, Sarah T. Dubb, L.B. Dunbar, Mia Hopkins, Cindy Kehagiaras, Angelina M. Lopez, Melanie Moreland, and Maria Vale.

Thank you to Livy Hart, Sarah T. Dubb, Heather Williams, and Destany Pingle for reading early versions of this story. Thank you to my editor, Beth Lawton. And thank you to every single one of you for reading this story. It means the world to me.

Love always,

Jess

ABOUT THE AUTHOR

Jess K. Hardy is an award-winning, bestselling author of contemporary and sci-fi romance. Jess writes about characters at any age, but especially over 40, finding second chances, proving that life, and love, only get better with time. She has ben featured in Publisher's Weekly and People.

ALSO BY JESS K HARDY

SPACE CRUISE ROMANCE SERIES
SUNASTARA & THE VENUSIAN
ELANIE & THE EMPATH

BLUEBIRD BASIN ROMANCE SERIES
COME AS YOU ARE
LIPS LIKE SUGAR
WISH YOU WERE HERE

THE CURSE OF NONA MAY TAYLOR

www.ingramcontent.com/pod-product-compliance
Lightning Source LLC
Chambersburg PA
CBHW071751150726
47998CB00005B/1890